"You sound more and more like my brothers every minute, and you've only been here a day," Keira said. "I hate to think what you'll be like after a month."

"Maybe it won't take that long to solve the murder," Nick said. "I'm going to want a DNA sample from your brother."

She scowled. "Why? He already provided one." Watching her partner's face, Keira made a deduction that was very upsetting. "Wait ... You ... think ... he ... falsified evidence?"

"I didn't say that."

"You didn't have to. implication. You want to take a sample yourself because you don't trust us."

When Nick swiveled to look at her, she could tell he was hesitant to say more. Well, he didn't have to. She knew precisely what he'd meant.

FITZGERALD BAY:

Law enforcement siblings fight for justice and family.

Books by Valerie Hansen

Love Inspired Suspense

*Her Brother's Keeper
*Out of the Depths
Deadly Payoff
*Shadow of Turning
Hidden in the Wall
*Nowhere to Run
*No Alibi
*My Deadly Valentine
  "Dangerous Admirer"
Face of Danger
†Nightwatch
The Rookie's Assignment

Love Inspired

*The Perfect Couple
*Second Chances
*Love One Another
*Blessings of the Heart
*Samantha's Gift
*Everlasting Love
The Hamilton Heir
*A Treasure of the Heart
Healing the Boss's Heart

*Serenity, Arkansas
†The Defenders

Love Inspired Historical

Frontier Courtship
Wilderness Courtship
High Plains Bride
The Doctor's Newfound Family
Rescuing the Heiress

VALERIE HANSEN

was thirty when she awoke to the presence of the Lord in her life and turned to Jesus. In the years that followed, she worked with young children, both in church and secular environments. She also raised a family of her own and played foster mother to a wide assortment of furred and feathered critters.

Married to her high school sweetheart since age seventeen, she now lives in an old farmhouse she and her husband renovated with their own hands. She loves to hike the wooded hills behind the house and reflect on the marvelous turn her life has taken. Not only is she privileged to reside among the loving, accepting folks in the breathtakingly beautiful Ozark mountains of Arkansas, she also gets to share her personal faith by telling the stories of her heart for all of the Love Inspired Books lines.

Life doesn't get much better than that!

THE ROOKIE'S ASSIGNMENT

VALERIE HANSEN

Love Inspired

Special thanks and acknowledgment to Valerie Hansen
for her contribution to the Fitzgerald Bay miniseries.

Recycling programs
for this product may
not exist in your area.

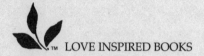

™ LOVE INSPIRED BOOKS

ISBN-13: 978-0-373-44477-9

THE ROOKIE'S ASSIGNMENT

Copyright © 2012 by Harlequin Books S.A.

www.LoveInspiredBooks.com

Printed in U.S.A.

Consider it pure joy whenever you face trials of many kinds, because you know that the testing of your faith develops perseverance. Perseverance must finish its work so that you may be mature and complete, not lacking anything.
—*James* 1:2–4

I never participate in a series
without thanking my fellow authors. In this case,
they are Shirlee McCoy, Rachelle McCalla,
Stephanie Newton, Lynette Eason and Terri Reed.
I'd also like to thank retired officer and author
Lee Lofland for steering my fictitious
police officers out of trouble as much as possible.

And thanks to my husband Joe and friend
Karen for proofing. Any mistakes left after their
reading are probably ones I made later!

ONE

*Consider the joy, my brothers, whenever you face trials
of many kinds, because you know that the testing of
your faith develops perseverance. Perseverance must
finish its work so that you may be mature and complete,
not lacking anything.*

James 1:2–4

Eager to get to work, rookie officer Keira Fitzgerald paused
on the stoop behind the Main Street police station just long
enough to stomp snow off her boots and fill her lungs with
the crisp, clean sea air of the Massachusetts coast.

The moment she stepped inside the building she sensed
an undercurrent of discontent that nearly stopped her in her
tracks. Something was definitely not normal.

Stripping off her gloves, hat and jacket she headed straight
for her brother Douglas's desk.

"What's going on? I haven't heard this much grumbling
since the Minutemen lost their last football game."

Captain Douglas Fitzgerald raised his blue eyes—a famil-
ial trait he shared with Keira—and arched his brows. "You'd
better go find out for yourself. The chief is waiting."

"For me? Why?"

"I'll let him tell you."

"Hey, I thought big brothers were supposed to look out for their sisters."

"Believe me, Keira, if there was anything I could do to get you out of this, I would."

"Out of *what?*" She sent a comical grimace his way, hoping that teasing would loosen him up. Instead, he merely shook his head and jerked a thumb toward their father's closed office door.

"Okay, okay. I get it. I'm going."

She smoothed her short, dark hair and checked every aspect of her neatly ironed blue uniform before knocking on Aiden Fitzgerald's door and peeking in. "Morning, Chief. You wanted to see me?"

"Yes," Aiden said. "Come in. There's someone I want you to meet."

Keira was duly impressed the moment her gaze swept over the man standing beside her father. Probably about thirty, he wasn't taller or more muscular than her brothers, and his hair was brown instead of Fitzgerald black, yet there was something extremely formidable about him. Maybe it was the way he studied her, his hazel eyes seeming to change to the sea-green color of his pullover sweater.

"This is Keira Fitzgerald, the officer I was telling you about," the chief said. "Keira, Nick Delfino."

Smiling slightly she extended her hand. "Pleased to meet you."

Although Nick accepted her overture with a firm grip he didn't return her smile. "My pleasure."

"Welcome to Fitzgerald Bay." Keira had to stop herself from nervously wiping her hand on the side of her uniform pants as soon as he released it. Not only had his handshake been firm, his warm touch had sent tingles zipping through her fingertips. She clasped her hands together. "Sorry. I just came in. It's freezing out there."

"Nick is from Boston. He's used to our climate," Aiden said. He cleared his throat. "He's been reassigned here to temporarily assist us in our investigation of the murder."

"The Olivia Henry murder," Nick added.

So *that* was what was bugging Douglas and the others. Their expertise was being challenged. No wonder she'd sensed so much tension in the air this morning. Nobody liked having their work questioned—especially not by some supposed hotshot from the big city. Then again, maybe they did need help. They hadn't made much progress on that case in the month since the body had been discovered.

Poor Olivia had been working as a nanny for Keira's brother Charles Fitzgerald, taking care of his young, motherless twins when she'd been murdered. The town was still reeling over her death and the senselessness of the killing, not to mention the undercurrent of unrest that lingered due to their inability to solve the case.

When her father didn't elaborate, Keira felt compelled to rise to his defense. "That's the *only* murder investigation we're working on. I assure you, Fitzgerald Bay is not a bit like Boston."

"I see." One corner of Nick's mouth twitched as if he might be laughing at them on the inside, even if he was too polite to let it out.

Aiden cleared his throat and Keira could tell that he was deeply troubled. It was natural for her father, as police chief, to take any serious crimes personally. She just wished they'd get this particular file closed—for everybody's sake.

"I'm teaming you up on the Henry case, at least for the time being," the chief said, looking from one to the other. He finally settled his gaze on Keira. "Nick is a highly experienced detective, which is the main reason I agreed to let him help us out. I had already talked to an old friend in law enforcement about bringing in fresh eyes so I didn't hesitate when I got a call from the State Police recommending we utilize Nick. I'm sure he can teach us plenty."

Her eyes widened and her mouth gaped. "But…"

"No buts, Keira. I'm speaking as your chief and as your father. When I partner you with any of our regular officers, especially with your brothers, I worry that they'll risk their lives to protect you."

"Of course they would. I'd do the same for them," she insisted, frowning and embracing Douglas's defensive mood more fully by the second.

"That's beside the point. You wanted to be a cop, so be one. You know this town inside out. You're the perfect person to acquaint Nick with everything he needs to know to conduct a successful investigation."

"Yes, sir."

Under other circumstances she might have given her dad a cheery, comic salute to encourage him and make him smile. This time, she cautioned herself; they needed to present a fully professional front. Three of her four brothers, Ryan, Owen and Douglas, as well as the chief, were members of the Fitzgerald Bay Police Department. They had a reputation to uphold. Particularly in the presence of this interloper.

"I already have my uniforms and lieutenant's brass," Nick announced. "All I'll need is a FBPD badge and I'll be set. I can start immediately if you want."

"Fine." Aiden produced the ID Nick had asked for, then dropped down onto his leather desk chair as if the weight of the world lay on his shoulders. "That's all. You may go."

Keira's cool glance met Nick's resolute one and held it for long seconds before she led the way out of the private office.

"I'd tell you I was sorry you got saddled with a rookie like me if I didn't think *I* was the one being picked on," she said over her shoulder as they proceeded into the main part of the station.

"No problem. You aren't the first partner I've had who wasn't particularly thrilled with me."

She couldn't help herself. The opportunity for wry humor was just too perfect to pass up so she sent him the most sardonically sweet smile she could muster and said, "Good to know. Add my name to that list, will you?"

Nick had been floored when the beautiful, dark-haired young woman had waltzed into the chief's office.

That was a *cop?* Not in his book. Keira Fitzgerald didn't look able to take adequate care of herself, let alone fight crime. No wonder her father had assigned her to him. At least that would keep her out of trouble. For now. If he decided that the whole department was dirty, as he'd been led to suspect, he was pretty sure the starry-eyed rookie would find that conclusion impossible to accept.

Yeah, Nick thought, remembering what had happened after his last successful assignment in Boston, *but Keira probably won't try to shoot me over it.* That was a definite plus in his book.

Briefings and his own additional internet research had shown him that the Fitzgerald Bay Police Department hierarchy was mainly composed of Fitzgeralds; Ryan was the deputy chief, Owen was a detective and Douglas was a captain, not to mention rookie Keira and the chief. Which one of the primary reasons Nick had been recruited by the Massachusetts State Police to conduct this undercover Internal Affairs investigation.

It wasn't going to be easy. Cops normally stuck together. Add the fact that many of these officers were blood relatives and you had an impenetrable barrier to the truth, particularly since Charles, the only Fitzgerald brother who wasn't on the force, happened to be a suspect in the Olivia Henry murder.

"Well, I suppose you want to get started right away," Keira

said, pausing beside a small, cluttered desk that Nick assumed was hers.

"Yes. I got here last night but I wasn't sure when the chief would want me to start so I left my uniforms in my room at the inn across the street. I'll go change and be right back."

"I may as well walk over with you. I can introduce you to the staff of the Sugar Plum Café and Inn as part of your orientation."

"Okay." He didn't care if she dogged his steps 24/7. The more details he observed and could put into his report, the faster he'd be done with this assignment and could get back to his regular job—starting with looking into a few of his old cases that were still nettling him.

Holding the front door for her to pass he said, "I'd like to begin with you, if you don't mind. I understand you were present when the body was found."

"Not exactly," Keira replied. "A bunch of us were at my father's house when we heard the call and headed over there. Olivia had been late for a lunch date with a friend, Merry O'Leary. It was Merry who spotted her lying at the bottom of a cliff near the lighthouse. We thought she'd just slipped and fallen until some men rappelled down there and could inspect the scene closely."

"It looked like murder right away?"

Keira shook her head. "Not exactly. Like the report says, at first glance we thought Olivia had fallen. It was the bloody rock nearby and the way she hadn't bled much after she landed that made us suspect foul play."

"How many bystanders had already tromped all over the evidence by then?"

Watching her face closely he saw nothing but honesty underlying her prompt denial. "None. I just told you. A couple men went down the cliff on ropes before we did anything else."

"Why take that approach?"

"When you see the area you'll understand. That was by far the fastest way in, and at that time we weren't sure whether Olivia was injured or actually dead."

Nick noted that his new partner shivered as she spoke and wondered just how much of a rookie she was. "This is your first major case?"

She rolled her eyes and tried to smile at him, failing miserably. "Oh, yes. The only death I remember ever seeing up close was a pet hamster I had when I was a kid."

She paused, swallowed and licked her lips, making Nick slightly uncomfortable for reasons he couldn't quite fathom.

"I refused to look in the casket at my mother's funeral," Keira continued. "I wanted to remember her when she was happy and full of life."

"I'm sorry for your loss, but having to deal with tragedy is part of this job. Surely you knew that when you chose a career in law enforcement."

That observation brought a smile back to Keira's face and a twinkle to her bright blue eyes. "Yeah, well… I'm afraid I pictured my job more as that of an understanding friend, kindly suggesting that lawbreakers behave themselves instead of having to exert authority over folks who have known me since I was a kid."

"Sometimes there are far worse problems to deal with, as you found out."

"I sure did," she said with a nod. "The hard way."

Keira appreciated the inn's welcoming beauty more every time she visited. Victoria Evans had kept the flavor of the old building when she'd returned to Fitzgerald Bay to take over the business, and most of its clients openly complimented her on the ambience of the inn and the delicious food served in the café.

Some locals had predicted that the long-ago sins of Victoria's father would keep away customers but that hadn't happened. Other than a few folks who still mourned for Patrick Fitzgerald, Keira's cousin, whom Victoria's father had killed while driving drunk, Victoria seemed to have overcome her dad's heartbreaking history. Even Patrick's most defensive kin seemed to have mellowed during the past ten years, although there was still a lingering touch of animosity that saddened Keira.

As Nick started up the gracefully carved stairway to the second floor, she called after him, "I'll wait right here."

And I hope I don't look half as uncomfortable as I feel, she added to herself. This was one of those times when she would have given just about anything to be free to turn on her heel and stalk out the door—without her new partner.

Unfortunately, it was her job to stick with the guy, to babysit him, so to speak. She could do that. She might not like it but she could do it. What was it that the Bible said in the book of James about withstanding adversity? Something about testing bringing maturity, if she remembered right. Admittedly she was only twenty-three and pretty inexperienced. Maybe this was the Lord's way of making her better at her job.

A shout and a heavy thud from above startled her out of her reverie. While other guests and employees froze and stared at the ceiling, Keira sprang into action.

Her boots thudded up the carpeted steps. What was going on? And why did it seem as if the whole inn was holding its breath?

I am, too, she realized, gulping air. The heel of her hand rested on the grip of her .40 Glock but she didn't draw it. No sense brandishing a gun if calming words would do the trick.

She reached the top of the stairs in time to hear another crash. And another. Then glass breaking.

Inching her way down the hallway she tried to pinpoint

the source of the sounds. There? No. Down there. One more door? Maybe.

Pressing her spine against the wall she stood to the side, out of the line of fire, just as she'd been taught at the academy, before readying her gun and knocking. "Police! Open up."

The door swung in. A man's shoulder and foot stuck out the opening for such a brief time they were hardly more than a blur.

Before Keira could swivel fully to confront him, he was jerked backward. The door slammed. She wasn't certain who or what she'd seen but she was positive one of the colors involved had been the sea-green of Nick Delfino's pullover sweater!

Hoping the door was unlocked she grabbed the knob. It turned! She was in. Almost.

Someone or something crashed against the door on the opposite side just as she was easing it open. The sudden jolt staggered her. By the time she'd regained her equilibrium, the door had bounced against the cracked frame and was standing ajar.

Keira gave it a shove with her free hand and peered inside. The room was a shambles. Its occupant didn't look as though he was in very good shape, either.

She didn't need police training to tell that Nick had gotten the worst of the brief altercation. He was half sitting, half lying on the polished hardwood floor, while examining the back of his head with one hand.

She directed the gun's barrel at the ceiling as she crouched next to him. "What happened?"

"Prowler." Acting groggy, he pointed to the open window. "That way."

"Will you be okay if I leave you?"

"Just get him," Nick ordered, rapidly regaining his senses and with them his air of authority. "Be careful."

A quick trip to the window let Keira scan the snow-covered alley, then lean out just enough to see what lay directly below. There was no one visible.

She raced downstairs, scanning the area and seeing no one but concerned residents. She ran around back. No one. With a final assessment, Keira rushed back upstairs.

"He got away," she told Nick as she holstered her automatic and reached for the radio clipped to her belt.

By the time she'd made her report and was ready to quiz Nick further, he'd gotten to his feet and was in the bathroom, washing his face and peering into the mirror.

Keira stood behind him at the open door, unable to keep from smiling. Except for a few bruises and a possible shiner, it looked as if her new partner wasn't badly injured. *That* was a relief.

Frowning, he met her eyes in the mirror. "What are you grinning at?"

"Just glad to see you're okay. How did he get the best of you, anyway? You look like a guy who can handle himself in a fight."

"A fair fight. He conked me when I opened the door. It would have been a lot easier to hit him back if I hadn't kept seeing two or three versions of him coming at me at once."

Nick blotted his face with a towel, then turned to her and crossed his arms. "Which reminds me. When you went to school, didn't they teach you to assume there'd be more than one perp at every crime scene? You came in here blind and didn't even bother to check the closet or the bathroom."

"I don't believe it," Keira said, astonished and more than a little chagrined when she realized Nick had a valid point. "I chase away a prowler and rescue you, and all you can do is chew me out for how I did it."

"I'm trying to keep you alive," Nick said flatly. "You can't let your emotions get in the way of common sense and training when you're on duty. The next time, that kind of carelessness might get you killed."

"I told you before. We don't have serious violence in Fitzgerald Bay. It just doesn't happen."

As Nick raised one eyebrow, he winced. "Oh, really? Tell that to Olivia Henry."

"That was a low blow."

"No," Nick said, shaking his head. "It was a fact. One you seem to be forgetting. If I were you, I'd be on edge every second until her killer's caught." He paused, staring as if he could look right through his new partner. "Unless you happen to know who the murderer is and you're not afraid of him."

"Why would I not...?" Keira's jaw dropped. "Oh, no, you don't. Forget any rumors that may be floating around town. My brother Charles is not only a doctor, he's a kind, loving man. Olivia was his children's nanny. That's all. He didn't have a thing to do with her death."

"Then prove it to me, starting by staying alert and on your guard."

"Against the murderer, you mean?"

"Against *everybody*," Nick said soberly. "Until we catch whoever hit that woman and pushed her off the cliff, a real cop would look at everyone as a possible suspect." His eyes narrowed. "Even her own brother."

TWO

Keira saw no reason to keep arguing with Nick about Charles so she decided to change the subject. "All right, I will admit I wasn't in top form when I came to your rescue. I'll do better next time."

That brought a chuckle she hadn't expected. He gestured at the ruins of his room. "Let's hope there is no next time. The proprietor will probably kick me out after she sees this mess."

"I was meaning to ask why you'd booked a room here. Wouldn't you rather rent an apartment, even if it's only for a month or two?"

He paused for several seconds before saying, "Sure, but where would I find one?"

"I think I may have an idea. I'll have to check with Douglas—Captain Fitzgerald—first. In the meantime, you'd better find your uniforms and make sure they're okay."

"Let's wait till your lab techs have processed the scene, shall we? I'd hate to disturb any clues."

Keira had to bite her lip to keep from laughing. "Our *what?*"

The befuddled expression on Nick's face finally pushed her over the edge and she did chuckle softly before waving her hands in the air and apologizing. "Sorry. I was just imagining what it must be like to have specialists at your fingertips, night and day. Around here we do pretty much everything ourselves."

"Okay. I get it."

"I don't think you do."

"Meaning?"

She hesitated in order to choose her words carefully, then explained. "Meaning, the Henry case. Like I told you, the minute we suspected we had a homicide we treated that victim and the scene with the utmost care. Everything was handled professionally, even though there was a storm brewing and Olivia's body was at the bottom of that steep cliff. Some of the evidence was probably affected by the fall, the surf and the weather but we did the best anyone could have. We're not hicks. We know how important it is to preserve possible evidence."

"I read the reports," Nick said.

"Then you also know we didn't write the parts dealing with the processing of the evidence. Everything went to Boston, with the body, for examination there."

"But you did investigate the whereabouts of possible suspects and check their alibis."

"Yes. So?"

Keira had assumed he was going to want to question a few persons of interest again but she was floored when he looked straight at her and said, "So, how can you be certain that everything in the file is accurate?"

"Of course it is. Why wouldn't it be?" she countered, bracing for another dose of his unwarranted skepticism.

Although Nick shook his head at her and appeared incredulous, he nevertheless answered, "Because not everybody in this world is on the up-and-up, rookie. One of these days you're going to take off those rose-colored glasses and see people for what they really are. Liars. Cheats. Self-serving hypocrites."

"It must have been really hard to work in Boston," she said with a tinge of sadness. "I'm sorry for you."

"Don't be sorry for me. Be sorry for all the nameless, faceless victims who never get justice because others decide to bend the truth for their own sakes." His pause didn't give Keira time to reply before he added, "Or for the sake of their friends or family."

That was another veiled accusation if she'd ever heard one. "Knock it off, mister. My family is innocent of any crimes, now or in the past. We're the good guys around here, in case you haven't noticed. My dad has devoted his life to upholding the law, my uncle Mickey is the fire chief and my grandfather is mayor."

"And three of your brothers are cops. I've never seen a town with more nepotism or more chances to sweep dirt under the rug than this one has. Look at it from my point of view, Keira. If you were an outsider, what would you think?"

"I wouldn't condemn people just because they're in a position to falsify evidence, that's for sure. My brothers would never be a part of any kind of a cover-up."

The rumble of his voice made the hair on the nape of her neck prickle when he stared at her and replied, "I sure hope you're right."

"I am. And once you've talked to all the people who were there and seen the truth for yourself, I'll expect an apology."

"If it's due, you'll get it," Nick said. "Nothing would please me more."

Nick welcomed the timely arrival of Captain Douglas Fitzgerald and one of the regular officers, a stocky guy named Hank Monroe. Monroe was a bit of a blowhard and thoroughly unlikable from the get-go but the captain seemed genuinely concerned about the incident.

"You didn't get a good look at the guy?" Douglas asked, his pen poised to take notes.

"No. Sorry." Nick was only half listening as he watched Monroe dusting for prints. "He was wearing a ski mask and a knit cap. I think he probably had on gloves, too. It felt like it when he hit me."

"Age? Weight? Distinguishing marks?"

Shrugging, Nick felt a muscle in his shoulder cramp so he kneaded it as he answered. "I'd have to guess by the way he moved. Maybe forties, maybe a little older. And he out-weighed me, although it was hard to tell if it was muscle or flab under his heavy black coat. Like I said, I was pretty groggy after he conked me."

"Any notion what he might have been after?"

Nick shook his head. "Not a clue. I don't think he'd been in the room long because he didn't touch my suitcases or my laptop. Most of this damage was caused when we fought."

He could tell that Douglas wasn't satisfied but there was nothing he could do to remedy the situation—other than suggest that someone might have targeted him because he had come to Fitzgerald Bay to investigate the unsolved murder. It would be interesting to find out how many people already knew why he was in town.

"Okay," Douglas said. "If you think of anything else, you know where to find me. What are you planning to do for the rest of the day?"

"That's up to Keira." Noticing the other man's raised eyebrow Nick smiled and added, "I'd call her Officer Fitzgerald but there are so many of you floating around, I figured it would get too confusing."

"Sometimes it does," the captain replied. "See you later,

then." He touched the brim of his cap, nodded to his sister and started to leave.

"Wait, Douglas," Keira said. "Nick needs a place to live, especially now. How about renting him the condo?"

"Well…"

Nick could tell the other man wasn't particularly keen on having him for a tenant so he provided a way out. "Don't worry about it. I can stay here."

"That's okay," Douglas said, visibly relaxing as he spoke. "I converted an old flour mill down by the river. It's not fancy but I'd be glad to rent to you. Just got the second unit finished, as a matter of fact, and my sisters decorated it a bit."

"Sisters?" Nick eyed Keira. "Oh, that's right. There is one more sibling, isn't there?" He grinned. "Is she a cop, too?"

"No way," Keira said. "I wasn't supposed to be one, either. Everybody expected me to go to work with my big sister, Fiona, in her bookstore, but I had other ideas."

"Now, why does that not surprise me?" Nick said, sharing a conspiratorial glance with her brother.

"That's what we got for letting Keira tag along too much when we were kids. She was always trying to outrun or outclimb or outswim us boys." Douglas smiled. "And she did, too. More often than I care to admit." He reached over and playfully attempted to ruffle her hair as she ducked out of reach. "She's one tough cookie."

"You could have fooled me until I saw her in action," Nick said, figuring it was better to join in the teasing than to behave too stiffly.

To his surprise, the captain sobered as his gaze swept the messy room. "I don't like this. See that you look after her well, Delfino."

"Spoken as her brother or a brother officer?"

"Both," Douglas assured him.

One glance at Keira told Nick she was not happy with the

direction their masculine discussion had taken. That was no surprise. Her academy records had already told him she was smart as well as being a crack shot.

Although he understood her desire to serve in her hometown with other members of her family, she would have been able to pass muster in just about any department in the state. Given the way her brothers and father were trying to coddle her, perhaps that career choice would have been a better one.

Nick began to smile as he made up his mind how to play this. "Okay, if you insist," he drawled. "But only if she promises to keep saving my skin, too, like she did a few minutes ago." He held out his hand to her. "Thanks, partner. I owe you one."

Keira grinned from ear to ear as they shook hands.

It was not going to be a struggle to treat her as an equal, Nick decided. She'd worked hard to make it this far and she deserved the badge she wore so proudly.

He just hoped the rest of her family was as upstanding and honest as he'd already judged her to be. If, as he suspected, the Fitzgeralds were the only ones who had known why he was in town—to a point, anyway—then the ransacking of his room led straight back to them.

In that event, would it be foolish to rent an apartment from Douglas? *No,* he decided. Although Douglas probably thought he could keep an eye on Nick that way, there was a good possibility Nick could turn the tables and do a little snooping of his own.

There was an old saying he often thought of in situations like this. *Keep your friends close and your enemies closer.*

That motto had never failed him before. The hardest part of his Internal Affairs job was telling the difference between his friends and his enemies.

After Nick had returned from a working lunch with the chief, Keira had spent the rest of the afternoon listening as

Nick casually interviewed her brothers Ryan and Douglas, plus Hank Monroe, mainly because they happened to be the ones he encountered in the office.

When Nick arrived at the station the following morning she jumped to her feet, more than ready to give him a promised tour of the town.

"How about driving around a little to orient you?" she asked before he had a chance to even remove his jacket. "I know you'll want to talk to some of the witnesses besides us."

It wasn't exactly comforting when Nick arched a brow and asked, "Why the big hurry?"

"It's not that I'm trying to rush you off," Keira said. "I just feel dumb sitting here like a barnacle on a pier piling and not accomplishing a thing. We've all been through this before. You've read the reports. Surely there's somewhere you want to go or someone you want to question."

"As a matter of fact, I've already talked with the lady who owns the inn and café and her staff," Nick said. "Last night, I had her move me into the same room Olivia Henry occupied when she first came to town."

"Why? I thought you were going to rent from my brother."

"I probably am. But I needed a handy place to sleep that wasn't a shambles and I also wanted to have a chance to go over the victim's former suite at my own pace. Didn't your department do that?"

Keira made a face. "I don't think so. It had been months since Olivia had stayed at the Sugar Plum."

"Still, there's always a chance she left something behind, either by accident or on purpose."

"Well?" Keira faced him, hands on her hips. "Did you find any clues?"

"No. But that doesn't mean I shouldn't have looked just the same. You never know. She did leave that letter to her 'Sweetheart' with—who was it? Merry?"

"Yes. I told you they were friends. That info is all in the file, too. Why do you keep acting as if we're either foolhardy or hiding something?"

"I don't mean anything of the kind," Nick insisted. He squared his cap on his head. "So, where shall we go first?"

The car Keira chose for their official use was a black-and-white, four-wheel-drive, short-bodied utility vehicle. Other than her personal motorcycle, which she'd had to forgo riding due to the snow and ice, she liked this unit best.

Right now, she figured it was important to acquaint Nick with her town, with the interesting if quirky residents, and get him used to patrolling these narrow, cobblestone streets. Unfortunately, he didn't seem to be paying much attention to her spiel or to the passing points of interest she was mentioning.

She frowned and quieted. All she could see was his profile. What was he studying so intently? And why did he keep peering into the side mirror that way?

"Hey. What's wrong?" she asked, surprised to see him twitch at the sound of her voice. Boy, when that guy concentrated, he really concentrated.

"Nothing. Why?"

"Because you keep looking behind us as if you think we're being followed."

His head snapped around. "Did you notice something out of place?"

"Of course not. Why are you so nervous? I wouldn't think catching a prowler in your room would upset you so much. Is your head bothering you? Maybe you have a concussion. Do you need to see a doctor?"

"My head's fine. Let's drop the subject of my fitness for duty, shall we?"

"Sure. No problem," she said, although what she really

wanted to do was insist he tell her why he was acting so edgy. Everything looked normal to Keira. Then again, she did see one strange pickup truck traveling in their direction about half a block back.

Disgusted, she shook off her misgivings. They crossed Oak Street, heading past the red-roofed old lighthouse keeper's quarters where her brother Charles and the twins resided. Keeping an eye on the reflections in her mirror she watched the nondescript truck turn and disappear down an alley.

See? There was nothing to it, Keira assured herself. So there were one or two vehicles around town that she couldn't readily ID. So what? That didn't mean there was any reason to jump at shadows the way her new partner seemed so prone to do.

Maybe he had personal problems, she concluded. If so, he'd come to the right place for healing. Except for the one recent murder—the first they'd had there in over forty years—he'd have absolutely nothing to worry about. Fitzgerald Bay was probably the safest town in the whole state of Massachusetts.

"I'll swing by Douglas's condo so you can see if it suits you," Keira said. "It should feel more like a real home than the inn does."

He shrugged. "It doesn't matter. Any port in a storm."

"Really? What kind of place do you have in Boston?"

"The usual."

The last thing he wanted to do was discuss his private life, not that he had much to talk about beyond his job. His Boston apartment was little more than a convenient place to crash. And the few romances that had crossed his path had always faltered because of his dedication to duty. At least that's what those women had each claimed when they'd broken up with him.

Nick glanced in the mirror for the hundredth time. His eyes narrowed. Could that be the same old truck he'd been watching a few minutes ago?

"Do you recognize the tan pickup behind us?" he asked.

"Not offhand, although I saw a similar one earlier. Want me to slow down so you can get a look at the license?"

Swiveling, Nick loosened his seat belt. "Don't bother. There's ice or snow plastered on the plate. I can't even tell what state it's from."

"I could pull over and let him pass."

"No. Keep driving steady."

"Why am I getting the idea this is more than curiosity on your part?" Keira asked, hands fisted on the wheel, eyes on the road.

"Just being cautious." He wasn't about to reveal the nagging notion that someone was already bent on stopping him from doing his job in Fitzgerald Bay. Whether he was dealing with a conspiracy or with an individual was a moot point. Danger was danger no matter who was behind it.

Of course, there was also a chance that his imagination was playing tricks on him. It had before.

Yet it was that kind of keen awareness of surroundings that kept veteran officers alive. He'd be a fool to laugh it off.

THREE

Nick was out of the vehicle the moment Keira came to a stop at the curb in front of the condo. Remaining close to the SUV he waited for her to join him.

"See anything now?" she asked.

"No." Although her position wasn't too exposed, it didn't suit him so he nudged her between himself and the side of the car.

"Then why are we skulking around? This is broad daylight in Fitzgerald Bay, not the middle of the night in some dark alley in Boston."

He forced himself to relax on the outside while his heightened senses continued their vigilance. "Look. Whoever was ransacking my room might have been no more than a run-of-the-mill thief. Or—" he cleared his throat "—he might have been somebody who knows why I'm here and intends to stop me, one way or another."

"Hardly anybody was aware of your assignment yesterday when you surprised the burglar, though."

"I'm not so sure of that. By the time I had a little chat with the proprietor of the inn around suppertime, she seemed to know all about me. She even understood why I wanted to transfer into Olivia's old room for the night."

"What can I tell you? It's a small town."

"Okay. So what if somebody is trying to convince me to give up and go back to Boston? Who do you know who might object to my being brought in to investigate the Henry killing?"

Keira chuckled quietly, grinned and arched her eyebrows at him. "Is that a trick question?"

It was frustrating to see that she wasn't taking this situation seriously enough. That was the problem with being raised in the same place she was sworn to protect. She liked it here so much that she was unable to see the worst, even when it was staring her in the face.

"Look," Nick said, "I know none of you are thrilled to have me butting in on your murder case but the chief did agree to accept my help so we may as well bite the bullet, so to speak, and make the best of it."

"Agreed."

"Good. That's a start. You also need to anticipate heightened danger once we poke our noses into other people's business. I don't think you're ready for that."

"We've been over this subject before, Delfino. What do you expect me to do, suspect everybody?"

"All I'm asking is that you keep an open mind in *both* directions, good and bad. Just because a person may be familiar to you, that doesn't make them innocent."

"Aren't you getting tired of hinting that my brother is guilty? I'm sure getting tired of listening to you."

"That's *not* what I meant."

"Sounded like it to me." She pushed past him and started for the condo. "Take my advice. You'll get along a lot better around here by keeping your unfounded deductions to yourself."

Nick followed closely, continuing to scan the area. "Noted. Look, Keira, I'm not oblivious to your family conflict. I'll back your decision if you ask to be reassigned." To his astonishment he saw her set her jaw and start to shake her head.

"Uh-uh. Not on your life. You're supposed to be the best. I not only want to learn from you, I want to be in on solving poor Olivia's murder. She didn't deserve to die, and whoever is responsible needs to pay. Scripture says that vengeance is the Lord's but I'd be overjoyed to have Him use me—use us—to bring that killer to justice."

"I believe you," Nick said, smiling in spite of himself. "You're quite a woman."

"I'm a *cop*," she countered, chin lifted proudly. "That's what I was born to be and that's all that matters right now. We'll get along fine as long as you add that important fact to the list of other things I've told you."

"Yes, ma'am," he said with a snappy salute.

"Humph." Keira made a fist and slugged him playfully on the upper arm while exhibiting a lopsided smile. "I'm glad we understand each other. Remember, I grew up with four brothers. If I could hold my own with them, I can certainly keep up with you."

She produced a key. "Come on. Let's have a look at the apartment. I think you'll like it."

As Keira unlocked the front door of the former flour mill, he studied the old stone building. It had two visible stories, indicated by parallel rows of multipaned windows. The idle wooden waterwheel had been left in place on one side and definitely increased the rustic structure's character.

Several cars were inching past, obviously taking it easy because of the slick roadways and the hidden hazards presented by the cobblestones beneath the packed snow and ice.

At first, Nick didn't notice anything odd. Then, in the background, he spotted a truck that looked like the one that had been following them before. It was parked in a private driveway with only the front part of its hood visible from behind a board fence. Clouds of rising exhaust indicated that the motor was running.

He tapped Keira's shoulder. "Wait. Look. Do you see what I see?"

She wheeled. "Where?"

"There. Half a block south. By the yellow house."

"That property belongs to the Smiths. They always go away for the winter."

"Any chance they're home now?"

"No. Their nephew sometimes stops by to check the place but he drives a red SUV so that's not him, either."

"Only one way to find out for sure what's going on, then." Nick was scanning the surrounding area. "It's too open right around here. What's the best way to work my way there on foot without being spotted?"

"The mill basement joins up with a river that's probably still frozen solid. We could travel along the banks until we got to some cover, then cut through a few backyards and come up behind him."

"Not *we. I,*" Nick said firmly.

"But…"

"No buts, rookie. I'll need you to keep an eye on that truck and provide a distraction if necessary."

"Okay, okay," she finally said with a sigh. "Come on. I'll show you through to the back."

Nick followed her. The vacant apartment was sparsely furnished yet appealing. Crossing the polished, wood-floored living space they hurried through the kitchen to a door that led them down a dusty flight of stairs into the former grain-storage area. The cavernous, musty-smelling room served as a catchall for extra building supplies and some antiquated milling equipment.

Keira threw a dead bolt and slid open a heavy, wooden, garage-type door. She pointed. "Head that way. It's a little steep but not bad. Once you reach the river, keep off the ice just in case it's starting to melt."

Nick might have rolled his eyes at her if she hadn't looked so apprehensive. Truth to tell, he'd been skating on figurative thin ice ever since he'd taken that first IA assignment and had begun to seek out and expose crooked cops—the kind who gave the whole profession a bad name.

"I know enough to keep from breaking through the ice," he said wryly.

"Sorry. Be careful, okay?"

"I will." He pointed back up at the living area they had just passed through. "Turn on a light in there so it looks like I'm making myself at home, then go back out to the patrol car and be ready for a pursuit if it comes to that."

"Gotcha." She reached for her belt, unclipped a small leather case and handed it to him. "Here. There's a base radio in the car so you can take mine."

"Thanks. Call me if he makes the slightest move. And don't look so grim. I won't get lost."

"See that you don't."

Glad that he'd thought to order her back to the SUV where she'd be safe, he clipped the handheld radio to his belt and started off at a jog. The way he saw it, the less Keira was exposed to added risk, the better he'd feel.

The thought of what her reaction would be if he actually said as much made him smile. Admittedly, his initial judgment of her capabilities had been too low but she was still far too green to be considered reliable, at least in his professional opinion. Many a rookie had learned the hard way that real life on the streets wasn't the same as acing tests in a classroom. Keira Fitzgerald was one cop he wanted to see get her seasoning without being hurt along the way.

Or disillusioned, he added. He didn't know what she'd do if her brother Charles turned out to be a murderer.

* * *

Racing back up the stairs and into the living room, Keira flipped a light switch on the wall and raised the blinds so any observer would be sure to notice occupancy. Using the side of her fist she wiped condensation off the window pane and peered out.

The tan truck remained parked where it had been, still puffing exhaust. What she couldn't see was whether or not the driver had stayed behind the wheel. That didn't really matter. If Nick radioed for help, and she prayed he wouldn't have to, she'd be back in the patrol car, waiting and watching, just as he'd ordered.

Checking the readiness of her Glock she holstered it and headed for the street. The trick was to appear nonchalant in case she was being watched. Part of her kept insisting she was being silly while the part that had listened to Nick's warnings shivered and surreptitiously scanned her surroundings.

Her jaw dropped when she noticed a crouching figure working his way closer, moving from shrub to shrub in nearby yards. Her initial reaction provided a jolt of adrenaline. Then, she realized who and what she was seeing.

Nick? It *was* him! The man must have run all the way in spite of the slippery riverbanks. And, judging by the darker-looking knees and ankles of his uniform, he hadn't made the trip without getting wet.

Proceeding slowly and taking extra care to avoid staring at Nick, Keira rounded the patrol car and started to open the driver's door.

In the distance a motor revved. The tan truck they'd been watching was not moving but a different one, a slightly lighter-colored one, was coming toward them from the opposite direction.

Keira reached for her belt out of habit, intending to alert Nick. Of course, there was no radio clipped there. She'd given it to him because he hadn't picked one up for himself at the station.

Muttering to herself she quickly slid into the SUV and picked up the mike. He didn't have a call sign so she simply used his name. "Nick. Come in."

Although he was now hidden from her sight she peered out at the area where she'd last seen him and tried again. "Delfino. Do you copy?"

Still no reply. The hair at the nape of Keira's neck prickled. Where could he be? Why wasn't he answering? Only moments ago he'd been working his way closer, so what was keeping him from using his radio? Had something bad happened to him or was he simply observing radio silence because of his present position?

If she spent too much time trying to reach Nick or called him on a different frequency, their dispatcher would surely get involved. Right now, that was the last thing she wanted.

In Keira's view, this incident with the truck was probably either a simple case of mistaken identity or her new partner was making a mountain out of a molehill. Being around a guy like him was going to take some getting used to. What a pity he was so uptight all the time. Life couldn't be much fun when he never relaxed.

And speaking of relaxing, she wasn't going to be able to dial back her own anxiety until her partner responded. She keyed the mike again. "Delfino? Come in?"

What she wanted to do was add, "Don't make me come out there and get you," like a mother chiding an unmanageable child, but she restrained herself. He'd be fine. He was a seasoned detective. And, after all, this was Fitzgerald Bay.

Clouds of Nick's breath condensed in the icy air as he panted, hunched over, hands resting on his knees. A dog barked in the background. Gulls circled and called in the cloudy, grayish sky, concentrating most of their attention on the wharf and the shoreline.

The driveway where he'd last spotted the truck was only a few houses away. To his left was the condo and the police vehicle where Keira waited. So far, so good.

Dropping into a crouch he began to work his way closer to the idling tan truck. *Almost there.*

Suddenly, the engine roared. Rear tires spinning in the partially melted snow threw icy, gray rooster tails off both sides.

Nick dodged behind the trunk of a tree, peering out in time to see the truck gain traction and slew into the street. It was too late to identify the driver or get even a glimpse of the rear license plate.

His shoulders slumped. Looking toward Keira he saw her standing beside the open door of the SUV and waving something. Nick knew it was the microphone to the police radio because the spiraling black cord stood out against the vehicle's white door panel.

Confused, he checked the handheld unit she'd given him when they'd split up. *Oops.* He'd meant to switch it to vibrate so it wouldn't sound off when he was sneaking up on the truck and he'd apparently turned it all the way off, instead.

Nick displayed it and gave an exaggerated shrug as he approached her. "Sorry."

"You should be. I was about to call out the marines." She gestured in the direction the truck had gone. "So, did you get a good look at him?"

"No. How about you?"

"Me? I was cooling my heels just like you'd ordered. I did try to radio when I spotted a similar truck." She was checking the area as she spoke. "It's long gone now."

"Well, that's that."

He was starting to get into the passenger side of the SUV

when a loud motor caught his attention. He paused and pointed. "You mean *that* truck?"

"Where? I don't see…" Keira put one foot inside the car and stepped up to gain a higher vantage point, using the open door for balance.

"Get in!" Nick shouted.

Although Keira did lean down and look at him to ask, "Why?" she didn't slide into place behind the wheel the way he'd hoped she would.

There was no time to argue. Or to explain. He grabbed a fistful of her jacket and yanked, pulling her off her feet and getting most of her inside with him before the second truck raced past and clipped the half-open door.

Keira yelped.

Metal sliding against metal screeched for a split second.

Nick gathered her up and held tight in spite of the way she was pushing him away. "Stop struggling," he ordered. "Are you all right?"

"I think so." He noted her grimacing as she tried to right herself. "I didn't get my foot all the way inside before he hit us but it's okay. I don't suppose you were able to ID that driver, either."

"No. I was too busy saving your hide, and we shouldn't go in pursuit until we get the okay on the safety of this damaged vehicle."

"Then I guess that makes us even in the rescue department. You can let go of me now."

Nick wondered if she could hear the pounding of his heart. He certainly could. It took immense effort to convince himself to release her and let her slide away.

The crestfallen expression on Keira's face led him to anticipate her quandary. "Do you want me to call it in?"

"No. I'll do it." Her lips were pressed into a thin line and she was obviously dreading making a report in which she admitted damage to department property while it was in her care.

Nevertheless, she gathered up the mike where she'd dropped it when they'd been sideswiped, checked frequencies and keyed it to announce, "Dispatch, this is unit four. All officers are okay after a hit-and-run but this unit's been damaged. We'll need assistance."

Nick listened to the ongoing radio conversation without comment. His partner was all business and sounded totally professional as she gave their location but he could tell she was shaking, inside and out.

Instinct told him to pat her on the shoulder the way he might have a fellow male officer. Good sense told him to keep his hands to himself and remember that his partner was *not* one of the guys—even if that was how she claimed to see herself. Good sense won.

FOUR

To Keira's chagrin, her brother Douglas and two other patrol cars arrived quickly, red-and-blue lights flashing. She climbed out to face the music, surprised when Nick stayed close beside her.

She'd thought, for a split second, that the captain might revert to his older-brother habits and hug her as they met but thankfully he restrained himself.

Keira managed a smile. "Hi. This time, Nick gets the credit for saving *my* neck."

Douglas arched a brow and scowled at her partner just the same. "Oh? Who was driving?"

"Nobody. We were *parked,*" Keira announced, waving her hands for emphasis. "Just sitting there minding our own business when a truck came along and sideswiped us." She made a face. "And no, we couldn't see who was driving or get the license number. But it shouldn't be too hard to find an old, light-colored pickup with part of the FBPD logo from that door stuck to his dented fender."

"Okay." Captain Fitzgerald turned to give instructions to the other officers before continuing to question her. "If you were in the car, what part did Delfino have in all this?"

"I wasn't totally inside," Keira told him. "Nick saw we were about to be hit and jerked me out of the way." Her smile grew naturally when she glanced over at her partner. "He's lucky I didn't slug him before I realized what was actually happening."

"Can you give us a better description of the truck? Anything? Make, model, year?"

"It was old and rusty," Nick said, citing a possible manufacturer. "Half-ton. Probably mid-eighties vintage, maybe a little older. The plates weren't visible. And the driver looked male, although I wouldn't swear to it."

"Okay." Douglas glanced past them to where Hank Monroe was gathering paint scrapings from the creased side of the SUV. "I'll check it over. Doesn't look like there's much damage other than cosmetic. As long as that door still latches you might as well keep driving it until we have a chance to send it out for repairs."

"This shouldn't go against Keira's record," Nick said. "It wasn't her fault. There was no way she could have avoided being hit."

"Noted." Douglas was eyeing Nick as he spoke and Keira felt compelled to defend him, as well.

"Neither of us is responsible," she said firmly. "We came here to look at the condo, that's all."

"There was no indication of trouble prior to this incident?"

She could tell that her brother didn't believe they'd had no forewarning so she decided to mention the other truck. "Actually, we had wondered if we were being followed after we left the inn but I don't think the guy who hit us was the same one we'd been watching, so I can't see any connection."

"Followed? Explain."

"That was my assumption," Nick said. "I noticed a vehicle behind us and because Keira—Officer Fitzgerald—didn't recognize it, we were on our guard."

"And?"

Agreeing with Nick, Keira said, "That's all there was to

it. We thought we saw that particular vehicle parked down by the Smiths' place so I loaned Nick my radio while he went to check it out. He'd just come back when somebody else decided to remodel my door." She made a disgusted face as she glanced toward the patrol vehicle.

"We've been talking about installing dash cameras," her brother said. "Maybe this will hurry up the process." Looking past her, he assessed the scene as he handed her his personal radio. "Here. Take this till you can get an extra for Delfino. Hank and I'll check the Smiths' place just in case there's any evidence over there but I wouldn't hold my breath."

"Unfortunately, I didn't get close enough to see much," Nick said. "I think that driver took off because he spotted me. I'm just thankful I was back here in time to help Keira."

"So am I," the captain said as he extended his hand to Nick. "Thanks."

"All a part of the job," Nick replied, accepting the friendly overture. "And while you're here I may as well tell you that I'll take the apartment—unless you've changed your mind."

"Fine with me." He quoted a monthly rate. "We won't need a long-term lease, will we?"

It didn't surprise Keira to hear Nick say, "No. I won't be here long," but it did take her aback when she felt a twinge of disappointment.

"What do you say we head back to town and grab a bite to eat?" Nick suggested as they drove away.

"Okay. Normally I'd suggest we eat at the Sugar Plum Café but in view of your recent hike up the river, I think it might be best if we went to Connolly's Catch, down by the marina. It's a lot more casual and the view of the bay is great."

"Suits me. You're driving. Is it far?"

"Not at all." She was grinning. "I knew you'd like the condo. It has everything a bachelor like you needs. No carpets to vacuum, a simple kitchen, no yard to mow, windows that overlook half the town and two restaurants within walking distance, including the one we're about to visit. And your neighbor is a fellow cop so there'll always be somebody to watch your back."

"What makes you think I need someone to do that? I thought this was basically a safe little town."

"It was. Until you got here."

He saw her shiver and decided to keep the rest of his thoughts to himself. After all, she knew about the murderer in their midst and if he mentioned that case too often she was bound to think he was attacking her doctor brother. That was the next person he wanted to meet, Nick decided easily. He'd encountered sociopaths who could skillfully hide their deviant behavior but most murderers were not that clever. If Charles Fitzgerald was half as normal as his sister insisted he was, he'd easy to figure out.

"Well, here we are. What do you think?"

Nick glanced up at the colorful, enormous sign above the seafood-restaurant roof while Keira parked. "Connolly's Catch. Interesting. At least it's not Fitzgeralds' Fishery or something like that. I was beginning to think there were no other families in town."

She led the way up the wooden steps and onto the porch before she paused to say, "I have to confess. Vanessa Connolly, the owner, is my aunt. She and Dad are brother and sister."

Nick smiled and politely held the door for her to pass. "Why am I not surprised?"

"There's one more brother in that generation, too. Remember? I told you Uncle Mickey is the fire chief."

"Right. Guess I'd better behave myself, then. You've got me surrounded. I think I'm going to need a program to keep all the players straight."

"You'll catch on. All you need to remember to stay out of trouble with my relatives is to assume everybody in town is kin. Well, except for the Hennessys and a few other families. Burke Hennessy will probably be Dad's chief rival for the mayor's job now that my grandfather has announced his retirement."

"Hennessy. Hmm. That name rings a bell," Nick murmured, outwardly directing his attention to the eclectic decor of the restaurant. It was New England kitsch and then some. Nets draped in the corners were dotted with blue-and-green antique glass floats. Harpoons hung crossed on the walls below paintings of whalers in longboats. The jawbone of a whale was suspended above the dining area and the tabletops were reminiscent of the worn plank decks of sailing ships.

"That's probably because Burke Hennessy was the first one to insist we should blame Charles for Olivia's murder and he hasn't shut up about it since," Keira said softly. "Don't believe a word that man says. I don't care what kind of political connections he claims because he's a lawyer—I wouldn't trust him as far as I could throw him."

She cupped a hand around the side of her mouth to add, "It might be best if you didn't repeat what I just said. I'm supposed to be impartial."

"Yeah. We all are. It's just not that easy, is it, rookie?"

"Nope. The more I learn about this job, the harder it gets, and the more I appreciate other officers. It's tough out there, especially when you can't tell the good guys from the rest."

"Welcome to the club."

Her pretend pout was so cute and so appealing he had to chuckle. Keira Fitzgerald might not be nearing the kind of job perfection she'd strove for but there were other aspects of her persona that were certainly endearing.

Not that he'd dare come right out and tell her so. By the time he was through working in her hometown, his name would be mud. In the long run, it didn't matter whether he judged her department to be innocent or guilty. He'd still be the undercover investigator who had had to lie to them all in order to do his job and that was the criteria they'd judge him by. In their place he'd have felt exactly the same way. Betrayed.

He breathed deeply, turning an intended sigh into a feast of the marvelously enticing aromas that surrounded them.

Keira stood on tiptoe to wave hello to a middle-aged woman with an infectious grin.

"This is Vanessa Connelly," Keira said as soon as she joined them. "Aunt Vanessa, meet Nick Delfino, a detective from Boston."

The older woman shook his hand firmly and regarded him as if he were an interesting specimen caught in one of the fishing nets adorning the walls, although he wasn't sure what he might be a specimen of. The minute she spoke, however, he got a pretty good idea.

"So, Aiden paired you two up, did he? My, my. Maybe he's finally taking some of my advice. It's about time."

"Nick and I are just working together for a few weeks," Keira insisted, "so don't start in on us the way you did with Douglas and Merry O'Leary, okay?"

"Hey, I didn't do anything. The good Lord made those two compatible, not me."

"Right." Keira rolled her eyes. "I've been telling Nick how great the food is here so we'd better grab a table. You never know when we might get a call and have to leave in a hurry."

"I'll take your order myself and put a rush on it," Vanessa promised. "The special today is clam chowder and crab cakes. How does that sound?"

Nick nodded and grinned. "If it tastes half as good as this place smells, it'll be the best thing I've ever eaten. Bring it on."

"Me, too. And iced tea, please," Keira said. "We'll sit right here."

Nick reached to pull out a captain's chair for her but she was already plunking down in a different one. Edging his own chair around slightly so that his back wasn't to the door, he joined her.

"Still nervous?" Keira asked.

"Still *careful*," he replied with an arched brow and a half smile. "I try to never sit where I can't see what's coming. It's an old habit."

"And probably a good one." Keira shifted slightly to make more room for him on her side of the small table. "This is the kind of thing I meant when I said I wanted to learn from you. My brothers and the rest of the officers in Fitzgerald Bay are much more relaxed than you are and I want to be prepared for anything."

Nick noticed her barely perceptible shiver. "Good. That means you're still open to new ideas. A lot of cops are so set in their ways they refuse to learn."

Leaning her elbows on the table to come even closer, she lowered her voice. "Actually, I want you to think out loud when we're going over evidence together. Ask me anything you want, no matter who it involves. Please?"

"If you're sure that's what you really want."

"I'm sure. It's possible that you and I can put our heads together and come up with another suspect, or at least eliminate Charles."

"And if we can't?"

"We will. I know we will. There must be something we're missing. Something that points to the real killer. You brought the murder weapon and the other evidence back with you since the lab was done with them, didn't you?"

"The bloody rock? Yes. And the victim's shoe. There were no usable prints on any of that stuff."

"What about the dolphin charm found near her body?"

"That may have been lost on the beach months ago, maybe last summer. There's no way to tell. And no, it didn't have any fingerprints on it, either."

Keira straightened to make room for the bowls of steaming chowder Vanessa was placing on the table in front of them and thanked the older woman.

Nick was glad they'd been interrupted. Of the two blood types found on the rock, only one had belonged to the victim. If Keira had read the lab reports she knew that, too.

Until he'd had a chance to interview more townspeople, he figured it would be best to limit their discussion of those particular clues. They led straight to her brother Charles.

Because her partner had grown so quiet and subdued while they ate, Keira decided to try to draw him out with questions. "I've been thinking," she began.

He slowly lowered his soup spoon. "Uh-oh."

"Very funny. I just wonder if maybe those guys in the trucks were only passing through. Either or both of them could have been criminals, of course, but maybe they had nothing to do with ransacking your room."

"Do you believe in the Tooth Fairy, too?"

"Okay, okay. You don't agree. Am I right?"

"For a change, yes."

His lopsided half smile pleased her beyond anything she'd expected and encouraged further banter. "For a change, huh? You sound more and more like my brothers every minute and you've only been here a few days. I hate to think what you'll be like after a month."

"Maybe it won't take that long to solve the murder," Nick said. "I'm going to want a DNA sample from Charles."

Now *that* was a surprise. She scowled. "Why? He already provided one."

Watching her partner's face, Keira made a deduction that was very upsetting. "Wait a sec. You think he—we—may have falsified evidence?"

"I didn't say that."

"You didn't have to. Nobody would mistake the implication. You want to take a sample yourself because you don't trust us."

When Nick swiveled to look at her, she could tell he was hesitant to say more. Well, he didn't have to. She knew precisely what he'd meant.

"Look, Keira, wouldn't you rather the second sample was taken and proved to be a match to the first? It would help the state police and your brother at the same time."

"The truth is in the first sample Charles gave."

"Okay. But Olivia worked for his family. There's still a good chance that some of the material found under her fingernails belonged to a Fitzgerald. The question is how it got there and whether that's all that was found."

"You have results that I don't know about?" Keira asked.

"We do have more than one blood sample from the rock that we believe was the murder weapon. Unfortunately, the blood type is a common one and it does match your brother's."

"I read that in the preliminary toxicology report. So?"

"So, the best way to clear his name is send a new sample for typing and a DNA test. If the prime suspect wasn't related to you, you'd jump at this chance. Admit it."

"Okay. Maybe you're right. But you're not going to pin this murder on an innocent man. We won't allow it."

"Do you actually believe I came here to frame him?"

Keira sighed. "No. But I've heard of cases where men spent years in prison before the truth came out and they were freed. Charles has small children to raise. He needs to be there for them, not locked up over some trumped-up evidence that an overzealous prosecutor decided to use."

"You're really afraid for him, aren't you?"

She knew Nick was reading her just the way he'd claimed he could. Well, maybe she was a little transparent but Charles was her big brother. She loved him. And she loved his twins, Aaron and Brianne, too. They were only two years old, their mother had deserted them, and now the nanny they'd grown attached to in her place had been murdered. What would happen to the poor little things if their daddy was hauled off to jail?

Before she could decide how to rebut Nick's suggestion that she was fearful, he reached across the table and patted the back of her hand. His touch was gentle and the look in his hazel eyes warmed her to the marrow in her bones.

"I promise you one thing," Nick said quietly. "I will never assume anyone is guilty unless I have solid proof. And I'll give your brother the full benefit of the doubt. That's another reason it's important to take a second swab for DNA. It's the surest way to rule him out."

"What if it doesn't? I mean, Olivia worked for him. Suppose she got his or the kids' DNA under her nails some other way? It didn't have to have happened right when she was killed."

"No, but she did have that day off."

"You don't know much about toddlers, do you? They don't understand things like days off. Maybe Olivia did something for one or both of the twins that day, even if she wasn't supposed to be working."

"I guess that is possible."

Keira was glad to see his expression show that he was seriously considering what she'd said. "Lots of things are possible when you open your mind and stop focusing on one suspect."

"Only after that person is proved innocent beyond the shadow of a doubt," Nick countered.

If Keira could have thought of a snappy comeback she'd have used it. Unfortunately, she knew he was right. Only God could be trusted to be totally fair, totally impartial.

That conclusion left her wondering why the Lord hadn't cleared her brother's name already.

FIVE

Nick didn't pay undue attention to the people standing near the cash register as he waited in line to pay for lunch. His glance strayed through the front window to the parking lot. Their black-and-white was visible. So were dozens of other vehicles.

He suddenly felt a jolt of excitement. There was an older, light-colored truck passing by!

A young waitress balancing a cumbersome tray of dirty dishes momentarily blocked his view. He dodged to peer around her and nearly upset her load.

In the few seconds it took him to help the woman regain her stability, the truck was out of sight.

Whirling, Nick was about to alert Keira when she raced past him and straight-armed the exit.

He slapped some bills on the counter, hollered, "Keep the change," and went after her. It didn't matter who the truck's driver was. Keira was far too quick to act without knowing all the facts. That kind of leaping to judgment was liable to get her hurt.

He'd left his FBPD cap in the SUV when they'd reached the restaurant so he shaded his eyes from the glare of the overcast sky. Where had she disappeared to? Even if she was hot on the guy's trail, she should have the sense to wait for backup.

One hand rested on his holster, the other reaching for the radio clipped to his belt as dozens of noisy gulls wheeled and squawked overhead, complaining about being disturbed.

Nick had been assured that working in Fitzgerald Bay would be a cushy assignment, a respite from the constant tension he'd been under in Boston. When was the so-called vacation going to begin? It certainly hadn't yet.

He keyed the mike. "Fitzgerald. Where are you?"

Two male voices answered almost immediately. Terrific. The whole force was about to find out he was separated from his partner.

He spotted a flash of dark blue moving across the deep piles of snow that had been pushed up when the lot had been cleared. *Keira?* Nick's pulse sped. It had to be her. Nobody else would be crazy enough to clamber across slick, uneven terrain like that.

Had she spotted the same truck he thought he'd seen or was she up to something else this time? With her, there was no telling.

In view of the trouble it might cause if he tried to radio again, he gave up and trotted after her.

Thanks to the slippery mounds of plowed snow, she wasn't making good progress. Considering all the unknowns involved, Nick was glad. Her reckless pursuit of a possible suspect, with no official backup and no idea what kind of criminal she might be after, was *more* than foolish.

Would he say as much once he overtook her? Probably not, although it was high time somebody put her in her place and that kind of sensible rebuke wasn't likely to come from any of her family members. If anything, they were overprotecting her to the point that she was worse off than she'd have been if they had yelled at her.

And speaking of yelling… "Hey!" Nick shouted with his hand cupping one side of his mouth. "Wait."

Although Keira did glance back at him, she continued climbing the piled gray drifts. They were packed harder than normal snowfall and far more slippery, as evidenced by the way she was having to use both hands and feet to crab crawl to the top.

She straightened and stretched once she reached the crest, apparently straining to see something on the other side. Suddenly, her arms began to cartwheel.

Nick watched her topple backward and start to slide toward him, headfirst, screeching all the way.

"Gotcha!" He caught her neatly by both shoulders and righted her. "Did you hurt yourself?"

"Only my pride." She grimaced and glanced toward the restaurant. "I'm glad my aunt didn't see me skiing on my back pockets or I'd never live it down."

"I won't breathe a word about it as long as you behave yourself in the future."

"I haven't been misbehaving. I just thought I could get a better vantage point from higher ground."

"You left your partner without letting him know and went off on a tangent all by yourself. Don't do that again, with me or with anybody else."

"Yes, sir."

Nick wasn't positive she took that promise seriously enough but considering the necessity of winning her confidence in order to accomplish his objectives regarding the Internal Affairs investigation, he figured he'd better lighten up.

"I'm only trying to protect you and still do my own job," he said, starting to smile slightly. "I'd better, or your brothers will have my hide."

"Probably. Speaking of brothers, when do you want to visit Charles and take that new DNA sample?"

Nick glanced at his watch. "Would he be available right now or do we need to make an appointment?"

"He's been doing most of his work from his house since he lost Olivia and has no one to look after the twins regularly. We can stop by his place and see if he's busy. It's close by."

"Everything in this town is close by," Nick quipped. "If it weren't so cold out right now, we could probably walk back to the lighthouse almost as fast as we can drive."

"Uh-huh. I love summer. Did I tell you I ride a motorbike when the weather's nicer?"

"No." He smiled and shook his head. "But it doesn't surprise me. Nothing you do does."

"You sound as if that's a bad thing."

"Not bad, exactly. I do wish you were a little more predictable, though."

That comment made her laugh and he shared her amusement when she said, "At least you can always predict that I'll be unpredictable."

"You are one scary partner, rookie. You know that?"

"Yes." Keira chuckled. "And don't you forget it."

The trip from the seafood restaurant to Charles's home in the lighthouse keeper's quarters was over almost before it began. Keira paused behind the wheel before getting out. "Can I be serious for a second?"

"Sure."

She was glad to see her partner paying attention, unlike some of the members of her family who still viewed her as the baby of the clan.

"Charles has been through terrible trials. So have his children. Please be easy with him. He's really a gentle soul. And a patriot. He served his country as a marine."

"And combat left him with a permanent disability. That's why he walks with a slight limp. I know. I read his military records."

"You did? Why?"

"Because I need to know as much about everyone in Fitzgerald Bay as you do. Maybe more. Don't worry. I don't plan to grill him."

Keira jumped out and joined Nick as they proceeded up the walkway to the front door of the white-painted cottage. Like the lighthouse and the other small buildings adjoining it, the house had a distinctive red roof. The grounds were parklike, featuring neat lawns that invited summer picnicking and a boulder-edged parking area to accommodate the tourists who visited later in the year.

Before Keira could knock, her brother opened the door. Charles's smile was tight, yet he welcomed them. "Come in. Please. I assume this is the new guy I've been hearing all about."

"Yes. Nick Delfino, meet Charles Fitzgerald," she said, then gave her brother a customary hug.

Nick offered his hand. "Glad to finally meet you."

"When did you hit town? First I heard of it was a couple days ago."

"That's about right." Nick eyed the sitting room. "May I?"

"Of course. Have a seat. Can I get you coffee or tea?"

"Thanks, no. We ate at Aunt Vanessa's." Perching on the edge of a simple tan-colored chair that matched a sofa, Keira smiled at the toys scattered on the hardwood flooring at the base of an entertainment center. "Where are the twins? I expected to find them watching cartoons."

Charles smiled and began tidying up the toys. "I put them down for a nap."

"That's probably just as well." Keira folded her hands in

her lap. "Nick wants to ask you some questions." She hesitated, unsure whether or not to continue.

"And get another DNA sample," Nick said simply.

Charles glanced from Keira to Nick, his expression tight. "Was there a problem with the first sample I gave?"

"Just double-checking."

"Good story. I'd stick to it if I were you," Charles replied, sounding resolved and a touch annoyed. "Okay. Swab away. Like I keep saying, I have nothing to hide. I didn't hurt Olivia. The children adored her."

"How about you?" Nick asked pointedly as he prepared to wipe a test swab inside the doctor's cheeks before sealing it for transport to the lab.

Charles submitted to the test, then leaned back, crossed his arms and answered. "I liked her, too. She was good with kids. The twins are only two years old. They really needed someone like Olivia after their mother left. I did all I could to make it up to them but that's not the same as having a woman's care."

"You and Olivia never argued?"

"There wasn't anything to argue about," Charles insisted. "When Olivia showed up needing a job, she was the answer to my prayers. I still don't know how I'm going to cope without her."

"Do you have anyone in mind to take her place?"

He shook his head soberly, sadly. "No. Dad's housekeeper, Mrs. Mulrooney, helps out when she can, and some of the teenagers in town do babysitting, but that's not the same as having a regular nanny." He smiled at Keira. "I've even pressed my sisters into service in emergencies. Fiona takes to it pretty well since she already has a little boy, but I get the impression Keira would rather chew nails than act as a nanny."

"Hey, I like kids," she countered. "I just understand them

better when they get old enough to tell me what they need or want. Fiona's Sean is easy to handle."

"How old is he?" Nick asked.

"Six, going on twenty. He's had to grow up a lot since his daddy was killed in a fire. Jimmy Cobb was one of the firemen who worked for our uncle."

Nick stood, apparently preparing to leave, so Keira joined him. "Are we finished here?"

"For the time being," Nick said. He once again shook hands with the doctor. "I'll be in touch if I need to ask you any more questions."

"Anything that will solve this case and stop the rumor mill," Charles said. "As you can see from the empty parking lot, my practice has suffered. Whatever I can do to help, just ask."

"Now that you mention it, I would like to look over Olivia Henry's quarters. Did she live here with you?"

"Not exactly. There's a small, detached apartment in the rear." He opened a drawer in an end table, took out a key and passed it to Nick. "This will open the doors. Do you want me to go with you?"

Keira shook her head. "I know where it is. I'll show him."

She said a quiet, private farewell to her brother, then led the way outside. "Go to the left, around this house. The apartment isn't any bigger than her room at the inn was but it was handy."

"I take it she spent her nights separately?" Nick asked.

"Of course she did." That question raised Keira's eyebrows. "I don't believe you, Delfino. You just can't give my brother a break, can you?"

"Proving him innocent will do more for him than looking the other way, if that's what you mean."

Suitably chastised, Keira had to agree. She unlocked the door to the tiny apartment and stood back so Nick could enter. "We were going to pack up Olivia's things and give them to her cousin but nobody's gotten around to it as far as I know."

His search was brief and unproductive. The room contained a bed, bureau, small closet and little else. "I thought women collected a lot more stuff than I see here. I assume it's been searched and dusted for prints."

Keira nodded.

He scanned the room one more before saying, "Okay. Let's go. I'm done."

Locking up and quickly returning the key to her brother, Keira rejoined Nick at the car. "Well? Are you satisfied about Charles now?"

"He didn't appear to be lying, if that's what you mean." Nick tapped his inside jacket pocket where he had stashed the sealed tube containing the swab. "We'll know more after this is processed."

She asked, "How long do you think it will take?" She was not pleased to hear her partner chuckle derisively.

"It won't be nearly as fast as you see it done on TV," Nick said flatly. "Figure weeks if not months. There's always a big backlog and this case doesn't merit setting others aside."

"It would if I had my way," Keira said. She started the SUV and backed out. "Where to now?"

"Back to the station. I imagine your father will want to see the damage to this vehicle for himself."

"You would have to remind me. I'm really not looking forward to trying to explain how I wrecked a practically new patrol car when I was parked." She made a face at him. "Do you want to pick up your stuff from the inn and take it to the condo, while I'm facing the music?"

"I can wait. I'll need a ride, anyway."

"You don't have a car here?"

"No. I arrived by bus," Nick said.

"Okay. I'll have time to drive you back and forth." Keira glanced at her watch. "We still have hours left on our shift."

"It feels like we've been on uninterrupted duty for weeks instead of a few days. Hanging around with you in your supposedly peaceful little town has worn me out. If this is quiet, I'd sure hate to see it when it's not."

"Well, at least nobody has taken any potshots at us. I suppose stuff like that happens to cops all the time in a big city."

"Probably less often than you'd think. And if there are shots reported, we're usually far too late arriving on the scene to nab anyone."

"Have *you* ever been shot?"

Nick raised a brow and regarded her as if she had asked him an inappropriately personal question. Finally he said, "I was shot *at*. They missed."

"I'm glad."

"Yeah." He snorted a wry chuckle. "I was, too."

"Feel like telling me about it?"

"There isn't much to tell. It was dark and…"

"A dark and stormy night?" Keira interjected, grinning at the pun and hoping he'd appreciate her humor enough to laugh.

"Yeah. Something like that. Do you want to hear this story or not?"

"Sorry. I do. Go ahead."

"I was sitting in my cruiser in an alley, waiting for my partner to get back from a pit stop, when somebody with a high-powered rifle took a shot at me through the windshield."

Keira's hands clamped tighter around the steering wheel. "That must have been terrifying."

"It did get my attention."

"What did you do then?"

"I rolled out of the car, hit the deck and got ready to return fire but I never got the chance. The shooter had taken off."

"Your partner didn't get a look at him, either?" Although she had to keep her eyes on the road, she did chance a quick glance at Nick and noticed that his expression was anything but cordial. Apparently he hadn't gotten along with whoever had been assigned to accompany him that night.

"No," Nick said flatly. "Nobody saw it happen and there were no clues in the nearby apartment buildings or on the rooftops we searched afterward."

"Wow. You must have really made enemies."

"I wear a badge. Most of the time that's all it takes. That's what I've been trying to teach you, Keira. Until you know for sure exactly what you're up against, you'd better treat every call, every response, as if your life depended upon it. Because it may."

Keira knew he was right. Her mind was willing to fully accept his warning. It was her heart that struggled. She truly loved this town and the people in it. Thinking of any of them as evil went against the grain.

If she adopted Nick's attitude and began to look for—to expect—wickedness all the time, would it spoil everything? That was certainly a possibility. Her own father had been going through emotional upheavals ever since Olivia Henry had been found dead so no one was immune, not even a seasoned officer of the law.

That was one of the saddest conclusions she'd ever come to. She pressed her lips together into a thin line and stared at the road ahead.

"I see you're finally taking me seriously," Nick said.

Keira nodded solemnly, thoughtfully, before she responded, "Yes. And I wish I wasn't."

SIX

The first thing Nick did after Keira dropped him off at the inn was phone his former precinct on his cell.

"Delfino?" the desk officer remarked. "I thought you were long gone. What's the matter? Did you get homesick for the Rat Squad?"

Nick gritted his teeth and took a moment to compose himself before ignoring the slangy epithet for IA and replying, "Yeah. I miss all my old pals so much I can hardly stand it. Cry myself to sleep every night. Listen, is the chief in? I need to talk to him."

"He might be. What're you doing, anyway? I know it can't be on the up-and-up."

"Yeah, well, you ought to know, Reilly," Nick snapped back. "Put me through. I haven't got all day."

"Okay. Keep your shirt on." On the other end of the line Nick was certain he heard a mumbled curse and shuffling of papers. "Here it is. The chief left a memo. He said to tell you, if you called, that he had to go upstate for a few days and he expects to be out of touch. Wanna leave him a message?"

Nick decided it was prudent to hold off. There were only two men who knew he'd been sent to Fitzgerald Bay or what he was doing there: his former Boston chief, who had assigned him this undercover task, and the high-ranking officer from the State Police who had made the original request for assistance.

Leaving any kind of message, no matter how cryptic, was far too chancy. "No message. I'll try again later."

"Suit yourself. Listen, we've got other calls waiting and all the lines are full. We work hard around here, in case you've forgotten. If you really want to get in touch with the chief, I suggest you try emailing him."

"Thanks. I will," Nick said before hanging up. He'd have much preferred to speak to his chief in person, partly because he distrusted email and partly because he wanted to hear the inflection of the man's voice when he asked for more back-ground info on Aiden Fitzgerald.

The FBPD chief seemed to be doing his best to run a clean department but so far Nick had only scratched the surface of what was going on in the idyllic-looking community. If he'd learned anything in his years on the force, it was that things were seldom as simple or as unsullied as they seemed.

He knew only one thing for certain. A person or persons in this little town had committed murder. All he had to do was learn enough to solve the crime.

"So, what's he like?" Keira's older sister, Fiona, asked. They'd shared an evening meal of takeout and were straightening up The Reading Nook bookstore together.

"Kind of odd. Which reminds me," Keira asked, "did you get in that new thriller I asked you to order?"

"Sure did. Now stop changing the subject. I want to hear all about your good-looking partner."

Keira chose to ignore the all-too-accurate description. "Well, Nick can be grumpy sometimes."

"Like?"

"Like when I drove him and his stuff over to Douglas's

this afternoon. He wouldn't let me touch a thing, not even the carrying case for his laptop."

"Why not?"

"Beats me. When I started to pick it up for him, he pitched such a fit you'd have thought I was about to throw it into the trash."

"That doesn't sound normal." Fiona frowned down from atop a ladder she was using to reach a case of merchandise in the storage area of her quaint shop.

"It may be normal for Nick. He's actually not too bad to work with most of the time. He's just, I don't know, *different* is the word, I guess."

"My Jimmy was one of a kind, too. Sweet and full of jokes, but also braver than any man I've ever known. Thank goodness Sean takes more after his daddy than he does me."

Waiting at the bottom of the ladder, Keira relieved Fiona of the heavy box and set it on a worktable in the back room. "Do you want to talk about Jimmy?"

Fiona shrugged and sighed wistfully. "Sometimes I think I do. And then I'll recall a special time we shared and I can't help tearing up. I try to keep from doing that for Sean's sake. After all, he's only six."

"I'm sure he understands a lot more than any of us think he does."

"Probably. I keep his daddy's memory alive for him as best I can. Jimmy's friends from the fire department help, too. Sean loves hanging out with those guys whenever they'll let him." She began to grin. "But enough about my boring life. Tell me more about this special new man in yours."

"In my life? Ha! Nick Delfino wouldn't even give me a second look if he didn't have to work with me."

That made her sister giggle. "Oh? And what about you? Would you look at him twice?"

Keira blushed and raised her eyebrows tellingly. "At least.

Maybe *three* times if you really want to know." The warmth of her cheeks flared. "Truth to tell, I have to watch myself to keep from staring. He's the kind of person it's easy to look up to. Know what I mean?"

"Not *exactly*," Fiona said, prompting Keira to go on.

"It's hard to explain. I trust his judgment more than my own. There's something reassuring about the way he behaves. He's all business and I can tell he's thinking the whole time, yet there's also a side of his character that's personally appealing." She paused long enough to fan herself for dramatic effect. "I could really get used to having him around."

"Woo-hoo. Sounds interesting, little sister. So, how do you know he's not staying long? Is that what he told you?"

"He and Dad both insisted it was true. Nick's only supposed to be here long enough to help us solve Olivia's murder, period."

Fiona's brows knit. "Why *him?* Is he some kind of super detective?"

"Something like that, I guess," Keira said. "He's on loan from Boston. Dad said he'd agreed to bring Nick in after sharing his frustration with an old friend who apparently helped arrange it."

Pensive, Fiona started pulling books out of the cardboard box she'd just retrieved. "Since it's our father we're talking about, I'll buy that excuse. If Aunt Vanessa was behind it, I'd suspect more matchmaking."

"I know exactly what you mean. I took Nick to Connolly's Catch for lunch today and you should have heard Vanessa. Talk about embarrassing." She laughed quietly. "Of course, she was right about Merry and Douglas being perfect for each other."

Noting the melancholy look on her sister's face, Keira reached out and patted her hand. "Maybe someday you'll find another man as perfect as Jimmy."

"Never," Fiona insisted, "but thanks for the encouragement. Keep me and Sean in your prayers and we'll be fine." She began to grin. "And while I'm at it, I'll make sure to pray for you and Nick."

"Whoa." Keira waved both hands in front of her as if trying to erase an invisible chalkboard. "Feel free to pray for me. Or for Nick. Just don't go joining our names like that, okay? The rumors will fly, anyway. No sense adding fuel to the fire."

"Okay." Laughing, Fiona spotted her six-year-old son in the doorway and motioned him over. "If you're done taking out the trash, how about helping me carry some of these books to the front and put them on the shelves, Sean?"

"Sure. Can I use the ladder?"

"We'll let Aunt Keira do that if we need to reach higher," Fiona said. "Although considering how she used to get into trouble for climbing trees and falling out of them when she was little, maybe I'd better do the honors."

Keira grabbed a short stack of hardbacks and handed them to her nephew before gathering some for herself. "Don't listen to her, kid. Big sisters always pick on us younger ones."

When the precocious boy piped up with, "I want a sister, too," Keira thought she'd choke.

One glance at Fiona told her they were both trying so hard to keep from laughing they looked as if they were about to burst.

The following few days passed uneventfully. Nick was starting to feel more accepted by the other officers and staff of the FBPD and Keira had been the picture of sensibility since the sideswiping incident outside the condo. Although he kept waiting for her next slipup and guarding her as if she were enrolled in the witness-protection program, he was actually pretty proud of the way she'd begun to conform to his idea of a levelheaded, alert police officer.

"I'm glad you decided to attend the memorial service for Olivia with me," Keira said, further confirming his recent conclusions about her competence. "Half the town will be there and you'll have a chance to see how everybody acts under duress."

"That's the plan." Nick felt a smile lift one corner of his mouth and knew he'd better mask his self-satisfaction with humor if he hoped to keep his partner on his side. "I suppose you'd object if I stood by the church door and sampled everybody's DNA on their way out."

As he'd expected, she rolled her beautiful blue eyes. "You're terrible. It was bad enough when you insisted on re-testing Charles. Although you'll have to admit he took it very well."

"Yes, he did."

Thinking back, Nick recalled his impression of the doctor as being positive. It was easy to see why Keira and the rest of the local force had trouble considering him guilty of any crime, let alone one of violence. Everything about him seemed open and aboveboard, from his welcoming smile to his firm handshake and willingness to cooperate.

"I'm not going to change out of my uniform because we'll still be on call," Keira said, checking her watch. "I wouldn't have time, anyway. The service starts in less than an hour."

"Okay." Nick decided to outline his specific plans rather than have his partner raise a ruckus when his actions surprised her. He reached into his pocket, pulled out a digital camera smaller than the palm of his hand and displayed it. "I'm taking this with me. You won't see me shooting, I promise, but there are times when a picture can tell us a lot more than direct observation."

"You're acting like you expect me to pitch a fit." She

chuckled softly. "Actually, I think that's a great idea. Just don't go sticking your lens in somebody's face and embarrassing them, okay?"

"Okay. I understand Olivia's cousin Meghan Henry arranged this memorial service and burial after the body was released by the coroner. Do you know much about her?"

"Not a lot. She hasn't been in town for very long. She did rent a cottage down by the beach so I suppose she intends to hang around."

"Why am I getting the impression that there's more you want to say?" Nick asked, eyeing her and waiting.

"There is one more detail. In the interest of full disclosure, you should know that my father is picking up the tab for the mortuary and cemetery costs."

"Really?"

"Yes. Dad often helps people out that way, although he never makes it public. The Fitzgeralds have always used their money for the good of the community."

"I'm glad you mentioned it," Nick said. "Otherwise I might have thought it looked odd."

"For a privately wealthy man to assist someone who has special needs in a time of tragedy? I don't know why you'd think that's strange."

"You obviously do or you wouldn't have brought it to my attention," Nick argued. "Don't worry. I won't embarrass you by asking questions at the wrong time. But I do intend to stand back and observe, just as we've discussed." He stowed the little camera, picked up his hat and motioned to the door. "Shall we go? The sooner we get there, the more we'll see."

"You promise to be discreet?"

He drew his index finger over his chest in the shape of an X. "Cross my heart. I'll stand way back and use a zoom lens. That kind of thing is done all the time when we're searching for suspects. Just ignore me."

The reflection in the glass of the door they were approaching showed his partner rolling her eyes and arching her brows as if that was the most ridiculous comment she'd ever heard, so he asked, "What?"

"Nothing," Keira insisted. "I was just thinking how impossible it is to ignore you wherever you are."

"Is that good or bad?"

She was shaking her head and blushing as she answered, "The jury is still out on that one."

Fitzgerald Bay Community Church sat on slightly higher ground than the business district. Its tall, graceful white steeple was visible from just about everywhere in town and on Sunday mornings the peal of its joyful-sounding bells summoned the congregation.

Since she was still living in the family home with her father and their housekeeper, Irene Mulrooney, Keira lived close to the church and always had a front-row seat to the melodic Sabbath concert. Right now, she wished the bells were ringing to help lift everyone's spirits, hers included.

"Well, I suppose we'd better go on in," she said, squaring her shoulders and starting off across the parking lot.

Nick fell into step beside her. "Is this where you usually go to church?"

"Yes. Peter Larch is our pastor, although he's getting up in years. I don't know how much longer he'll be able to serve before his health forces him to retire."

"So, you'd say he knows lots of townspeople?"

Keira cast a wary glance at him. "I don't believe you, Delfino. You want to grill the preacher, too?"

"If it will help me do my job, yes. Nobody should be off-limits. If you weren't so close to the situation, you'd feel the same."

"I suppose I would. But for the present, let's stick to observing the mourners and keeping a low profile, shall we? Remember, this is a house of worship."

"I'm not likely to forget."

Keira was certain she saw him punctuate his statement with a barely perceptible shiver. "What's that supposed to mean?"

"Let's just say I'm not at home in churches," Nick replied. "Never was."

"That's too bad. Some of my fondest childhood memories are of sitting in this very sanctuary with my family. When my mother was alive, we never missed a service."

"And lately?"

"I attend whenever I can. So do most of my siblings. Dad and my grandfather aren't quite that faithful, although I guess I can understand why. There are still times when I can visualize my mother's casket sitting right where Olivia's will be today. That's a tough memory."

"I suppose it would be."

"What about your family?" Keira asked, hoping her own openness would lead him to divulge the same kind of confidences. "Are your parents living?"

"Yes. Last I heard, they were happily basking in the Florida sun. We're not close the way you are with your relatives. And I have no brothers or sisters."

"I'm so sorry."

It surprised her when her partner simply shrugged that comment off. Perhaps his lack of personal connections to others didn't matter to him. Then again, since he hadn't been raised around a big, friendly clan like hers, maybe he just didn't know what he'd been missing.

Or maybe he was the kind of guy who craved solitude. In view of their occupation and the fact that some folks viewed all police as their enemy, perhaps Nick had chosen a fitting career after all.

Keira stepped through the tall, carved wooden doors decorating the church's main entrance. The atmosphere inside was hushed, the crowd in the foyer larger than she'd expected, given that Olivia had resided in Fitzgerald Bay for such a short time compared to most residents.

Somber-faced for the most part, the mourners were nodding polite greetings to each other as they inched toward the guest book and took turns signing.

"That's Burke Hennessy and his family over there," Keira whispered to Nick, cocking her head toward a group entering the sanctuary ahead of them. "Burke is the older man with the receding blond hair."

"He has three children?"

Keira subdued an inappropriate snicker just in time to keep from embarrassing herself. "You mean including the tall blonde? Nope. That's his second wife, Christina. She's not quite young enough to be his daughter but almost. The younger guy is Cooper, Burke's son from his first marriage. I think he's about twenty-five. And the baby is Georgina."

"Cute little kid."

"I agree. She didn't get her beauty from her parents, though. They adopted her from a drug addict and saved her life, as Burke loves to remind people. He usually sounds like he's campaigning for political office."

"Then she's a lucky baby."

"Maybe. Christina likes to play at being a mommy but I expect the nanny to take Georgina outside before the service begins. Leave it to Burke to squeeze all the mileage he can out of the happy-family image."

"He's also the guy who keeps insisting your brother is guilty, right? Isn't that Charles over there?"

"Yes." Keira's shoulders slumped with disappointment. "I told him not to come today but he insisted that the twins needed to say goodbye to Olivia. Of course, they won't understand what's going on, especially not with a closed casket."

"That's probably for the best," Nick said. "I'm not sure it's wise to bring impressionable kids to something like this, anyway."

"I wonder. I was very young when my grandmother Fitzgerald passed away and I never got to see her after she went into the hospital that last time. I remember wishing I could have." She sighed heartily. "Oh, well, we'll meet again in heaven."

Although Nick quickly turned away, she noticed how uneasy he seemed. "I get the idea you don't share my faith," she remarked. "That's a shame."

"What is? That I don't waste my time looking for pie in the sky?"

"No. That you don't have an open mind. I'm certainly no theologian. I don't pretend to be. Still, I prefer to think that, even if I comprehend only the most tenuous elements of Christianity, it's still better than having no faith at all." She smiled slightly. "Does that make sense to you?"

"Not a bit."

Keira's smile grew. "That's okay. I'm not going to beat you over the head with my Bible."

"Good to know." Nick leaned closer and cupped his hand to speak as privately as possible. "I'm sure we'd garner even more attention than we already are if you caused a scene like that."

"I told you we'd start rumors by being seen together, Delfino. That's what happens in a small town where everybody knows practically everyone else."

She sensed him waiting behind her while she paused to sign the guest book, then led the way into the softly lit sanctuary. Candles flickered at the altar in front of a plain wooden cross. On either side of the room were familiar stained-glass windows depicting scenes from the Bible, primarily those featuring water. That same theme was carried out by old paintings of sailing ships leaving a port that Keira assumed represented the historical Fitzgerald Bay.

As she and Nick accepted the commemorative handout from the usher, she saw him staring at the blurred but lovely photo on its cover. Olivia Henry had been strikingly beautiful in life, with fair hair, blue eyes and a porcelain complexion, although there was also a certain aura of sadness about her that detracted from her ethereal beauty.

The notion of dying settled into Keira's mind. An unexpected shiver zinged up her spine and tingled the hair at the nape of her neck. She might easily have been killed when their SUV had been sideswiped.

Nick leaned closer. "What's wrong? Are you cold?"

"No. I was just thinking about the truck that hit us."

"Are you ready to admit that wasn't an accident?"

"There's no way to say for sure," Keira argued. "If it really was an attack—and I'm not saying it was—the driver might not have realized I was in the way. He might have merely meant to damage the car."

"Would you bet your life on that conclusion?" Nick asked. "Because if you're wrong, that's exactly what you'll be doing."

She might have whispered a witty comeback if she could have come up with one before the service began.

Music played softly. Then Pastor Larch spoke of Olivia's virtues and the sad loss of one so young while Keira's restless mind wandered. Even if she wasn't totally safe on the streets, she was safe sitting in church surrounded by people she could trust—especially the man beside her, she admitted with a twinge of both sadness and joy. Nick had only been part of her life for a few days, yet he was already the first person she pictured when she wanted to feel totally secure.

Logically, since Nick outranked her, she supposed she was looking up to him just as she did her siblings, although she definitely did *not* see him as a brother. Uh-uh. He was the kind of amazing guy who rode in on a white horse and rescued damsels from fire-breathing dragons or liberated them from castle towers where they'd been chained by ogres.

She hoped Nick didn't view her as his troublesome little sister the way her brothers often seemed to. How she *did* want him to see her was another question altogether. One she chose to consciously ignore for the time being.

SEVEN

Nick was surprised to learn that the interment of Olivia Henry's body would take place in the cemetery behind the church where so many Fitzgeralds and other pioneers already lay.

Sticking to the outermost perimeter and standing partially behind a tree for cover, he aimed his camera at faces in the crowd and began snapping picture after picture. Most would be useless, of course. If there were one or two that told him something he didn't already know, he'd be satisfied. At least the weather was better today. The sun was peeking through the clouds for a change. He'd had enough winter to last him a long, long time.

Merry O'Leary, a woman Keira had introduced him to in passing, stood with Fiona and Douglas Fitzgerald, who had his arms around both women and was comforting them as they blotted their tears.

Nick had to keep reminding himself that this was just a job—for which he was ideally suited—because his conscience was uneasy. It seemed wrong to photograph people who were clearly mourning, yet it was standard procedure, especially in murder cases. Often there was no other way to catch the fleeting clues that might eventually help solve the case.

There was Charles, with his twins, Brianne and Aaron. The man seemed genuinely bereft and was obviously trying to control his emotions for the sake of his young children. A slightly portly, older woman stood beside him.

Glad when Keira sought him out and joined him on the periphery, Nick asked, "Who's that lady over there with Charles and the kids?"

"Irene Mulrooney. She's the housekeeper Charles mentioned. She helps out by watching the twins sometimes, especially since…"

"Sorry. I have to keep digging."

"I know you do. What else would you like to know?"

"How about the Hennessy kid? Cooper, you said his name was? He looks as if he'd like to jump into that grave with Olivia. How well did he know her?"

"Actually, he claimed he'd dated her but it seemed pretty far-fetched to me. I mean, she was beautiful and strong willed. Look at Cooper. The poor guy is…" She cleared her throat. "Well, he's a Hennessy."

"Hey, he can't help who his daddy is." Snapping a few more shots Nick continued. "I think you were right about the baby's nanny being ready to take over. That's who that short, older woman standing behind them is, right?"

"Yes. Delores Nunez. She's been with the family since Georgina arrived. They also had a housekeeper until recently. Helen Yorke."

"Really? What happened to her?"

"Personal problems. And before you go getting suspicious of Helen, too, we checked her story. Her mother got sick and needed her, so she quit and left town."

"Have they replaced her?" Nick asked, snapping pictures as he spoke.

"I don't think so. It's a good thing they have a nanny. I understand Christina has trouble coping with her own daily life, let alone adequately managing a household and an inquisitive toddler."

Keira paused for a few moments then gestured with a lift of her chin. "See what I mean? If you don't want a child to play with your fancy jewelry, you don't wear any. Ever since Christina picked up Georgina again, she's had to constantly keep prying that jingly bracelet out of the baby's fingers."

"I thought I heard something like that making noise earlier." Nick smiled at her. "I'm glad it wasn't my imagination."

"It could have been God ringing the doorbell to try to get your attention."

"In your dreams," Nick replied. Scanning the gathering he began to scowl when he noticed how upset the police chief seemed. Aiden was trying to hide his emotions but anyone could see he was deeply moved.

That was sort of understandable since this death had happened in his town and on his watch, Nick reminded himself. And the young victim had been loosely attached to the Fitzgerald family, as well. Charles was clearly mourning, as were many of the others. Even Keira had swiped away a stray tear or two as Pastor Larch closed in prayer.

It must be comforting to think this wasn't the end, Nick mused, although there was nothing anybody could do about it one way or the other. When a person's time was up, it was up. Period. Besides, if these folks really did believe in heaven, why were they crying?

Continuing to snap pictures, he asked Keira that very question.

She smiled and sniffled. "We're probably thinking of ourselves. Just because we have a hope of spending eternity together doesn't mean we don't grieve. I still miss my mother almost every day. I'm sure Dad does, too."

"Sorry. I didn't mean to dredge up bad memories."

"They're not bad," she told him, sighing. "They just are

what they are. If I understood even a smidgen of God's plans for my life I sometimes think I'd be happier, but I'd probably also try to help Him and ruin the whole thing. Right now, I'm just glad I'm not in a position to ask Him about it face-to-face."

He gritted his teeth before replying, "Yeah, so am I."

"I'm restless after the morning we just spent," Keira told Nick as they left the cemetery. "Since the weather is finally nicer, why don't we visit the murder scene?"

"I thought you'd never get around to that." He grinned over at her. "The way you kept putting me off when I suggested it, I was beginning to wonder."

"Hey, the tide was either too high or there was a storm at sea when you asked before. I should have taken you down to the beach, anyway, and let you get swamped in those monstrous waves. It would have served you right."

"Why didn't you?"

She couldn't help laughing. "Because I didn't want to drown with you, if you must know. I've lived here all my life. I can read the bay the way you read the streets of Boston. I knew better than to go earlier."

"How do we get there? I'm not looking forward to rappelling down the cliff the way the fire department had to when they retrieved the body."

"Actually, Douglas helped, too. But we won't have to take that kind of risk. We can park near your apartment and hike in."

"There's a way to do that?"

"There is at low tide." She checked her watch. "We'll have time if we don't stop to admire the scenery or pick up seashells."

"Do you collect those?"

"I used to," Keira said, sensing a slight blush warming her

cheeks. "When we were kids we all spent a lot of time investigating the shore. My brothers and I used to plant clues to try to fool each other, then pretend we were real detectives solving real crimes."

She could feel Nick's gaze fixed on her so she laughed. "No. We don't still do that if that's what you're thinking."

"I never said a word."

"You didn't have to. I can see it on your face. Believe me, if there was anything on that beach where Olivia was found, it didn't come from one of us."

Although he didn't answer, she was satisfied that he'd accepted her claim. He'd better. Thanks to Burke Hennessy and a few other folks who'd sided with him, there had already been enough false accusations directed toward her family.

She didn't expect Nick to find anything else on the rocky shoreline below the cliff where the lighthouse stood, but if it would help him visualize the crime scene better, she had no objection to guiding him. It would be the first time she'd set foot down there since the summer before Olivia's murder and she wasn't looking forward to it.

However, she was also a good cop. She'd go anywhere necessary in order to do her job and solve crimes.

Specific, painful memories had been revived during the church service earlier. She could vividly recall the sight of the body being hoisted from the rocks below as she and others who were waiting on the cliff top had prayed that the identity of the victim was a mistake. It still seemed unbelievable that someone as young and full of life as Olivia had actually died. If she had merely fallen...

But she hadn't, Keira reminded herself. Forensics had confirmed that someone had hit her over the head with a rock then shoved her off that cliff and thrown the bloody murder weapon down after her. Given the nor'easter that had been imminent at that time, it was possible the killer had thought her body would wash out to sea and never be found.

Had God intervened? Keira asked herself. Was He the reason Merry had happened upon the scene in time to stop the storm-tossed waves from taking Olivia?

She chanced a sidelong glance at her partner. An even more interesting question was why Nick Delfino had been the one chosen to come to Fitzgerald Bay to assist in the investigation. In the deepest recesses of her mind lurked the suspicion that she had been destined to meet him, one way or the other, and his presence was all a part of God's divine plan.

Or a big cosmic joke, she countered, feeling silly. That was far more likely.

Nevertheless, she couldn't totally erase the notion that having Nick around had been advantageous—and not only when he'd protected her.

She sensed his eyes on her. Her head snapped around. "What?"

"I was just wondering why you looked so pleased with yourself all of a sudden."

"Did I? I was probably thinking about getting out and burning some excess energy hiking along the shore," Keira said, hoping her reddening cheeks weren't giving her away.

"I don't suppose there's any chance we could drive down there?"

"Sorry. No. It's too rocky, even when the tide is out. When the water's high we could probably approach in a small boat, but then the murder site would be underwater."

"Okay. I get the idea. We have to walk. I'll cope."

"What a trouper," Keira teased. She pulled into the driveway of the old mill and stopped. "Ready?"

"As ready as I'll ever be. You're the native. Is there anything special I need to take along?"

"A little food for quick energy wouldn't hurt." She was watching him carefully scan their surroundings the way he always did and it gave her the willies. "You haven't seen signs of any suspicious trucks, have you?"

"Nope. I imagine they either left town or decided to lie low."

She headed for the front door. "Suits me. Let's go grab a snack. I know where Douglas keeps the granola bars."

"I thought you said we were going to take *food*."

"Spoken like a typical man," Keira countered with a comical grimace. "I'll see if I can find you some beef jerky to gnaw on if you want. Do you have any snacks at your place we can grab easily?"

When she noticed his hesitation and the way his smile quickly faded it made her curious. "What's the matter? Did you forget to tidy up this morning? I don't care if you throw your dirty socks on the floor or leave stacks of dishes in the sink."

"It's not that. I just haven't stocked the cupboards yet," Nick said flatly. "Grab whatever you need from your brother's place and let's get going."

"Okay, okay. Keep your shirt on."

"You don't need a key?" he asked, following her into an apartment that was the mirror image of his own, although it did look a lot more homey and lived-in.

"A key? Why? We hardly ever lock our doors around here."

"That seems rather foolish."

"Not to us. We trust each other." Sizing up his posture and tight expression, she huffed. "Yeah, I know. We shouldn't be so easygoing. It's really depressing to think that."

"Maybe, after the murder is solved, you'll all be able to settle down to the peaceful lives you used to enjoy."

"I hope so."

Stuffing packages of granola bars into her jacket pockets, Keira took a deep breath and released it as a sigh. "At this point, I wonder if we may have lost our peace and tranquility for good."

Nick would have invited Keira to raid his fridge if he hadn't remembered leaving a folder filled with sensitive documents lying on the kitchen table where she might have noticed and asked about it.

In retrospect, he knew he should have either locked up that inside information or tucked it into his laptop case to take to work with him.

Logic had insisted that his personal research into Fitzgerald Bay would be more secure from prying eyes at the condo, particularly since no one suspected he was working undercover. At least not yet. What he hadn't anticipated was Keira deciding to stop by without warning.

They exited via the basement door, just as he had when he'd followed the river upstream. In this case, however, she turned south and led the way past rocky outcroppings, skirting the largest ones by sticking close to the lapping water.

Nick could tell from the wet rocks and sand that the tide had recently receded. How long would it be before the waves rose again? He wasn't looking forward to getting an unnecessary shower of icy seawater. Perhaps that was why his partner seemed to be moving so rapidly.

"Hey," he called after her. "What's the hurry? Are we racing the tide?"

"No. Sorry. I tend to get carried away sometimes."

When Keira grinned and turned to wait for him to catch up, Nick was struck by how different she looked. Wisps of her silky, dark hair had been caught in the sea breeze and were tickling her forehead below the brim of her cap. Her eyes sparkled more brightly than a summer sky and her cheeks held the rosy, healthy glow of someone who belonged to the rock-strewn Atlantic coast as surely as the other flora and fauna did. Keira Fitzgerald was the essence of New England's hearty stock, totally in her element and overflowing with the joy of having found her ideal niche.

Moreover, Nick realized, it was a distinct pleasure to be there with her. The freedom and lack of pretense she exhibited was catching. He, too, felt more lighthearted.

"How much farther is it?" he asked when he jogged up beside her.

"Just around the next big rockfall," Keira said, pointing. "This part of the bay hasn't changed since I was a kid. I know it like the back of my hand."

"Since you were a kid? You mean last year?" Nick teased.

"Hey, just because you're an old curmudgeon, that doesn't give you the right to pick on me. How old are you, anyway?"

"Thirty, going on a hundred, at least," he replied.

Scaling a boulder that blocked their path, he almost forgot himself and automatically reached for her hand to help her climb.

That was the kind of gut-level reaction that would get him into plenty of trouble, he knew, yet at that moment, on that deserted stretch of shoreline, it seemed perfectly natural. He couldn't explain it. He simply knew that he and Keira were in sync in ways that were foreign to him.

Did she feel the same unspoken connection? Nick wondered. With her, it was impossible to tell. Unless she was berating him for suspecting her brother or trying to convince him that she didn't need protecting, she was always upbeat. At least, that was the impression he'd gotten.

Even at the funeral? he asked himself.

To his surprise and chagrin he had to answer in the affirmative. It wasn't so much that Keira was carefree. She had certainly empathized with everyone's feelings of loss. She was simply comfortable in her own skin, with her personal beliefs, and for that he envied her.

EIGHT

"You can't see the lighthouse from here but I know this is the spot," Keira shouted, cupping a hand around her mouth so she could be heard over the raucous screeching of the gulls and the drumming, humming echo of the surf.

Most of the seabirds were launching themselves from the steep precipice above or diving for food in the shallows. A few waddled along the shoreline like hungry diners at a sumptuous buffet, picking up whatever tasty tidbits the ocean had recently deposited and squabbling over the smallest morsel.

"It's right above us?" Nick asked.

Keira nodded. "Yes. And over here is where they found Olivia. If she hadn't lost a shoe at the top of the cliff, Merry might never have thought to look for her down here."

"I saw that in the report."

Standing back to observe, Keira watched Nick skirt the scene before cautiously approaching. There was nothing visual left from the murder, of course. Not after several storms and the usual high tides. Still, he was looking at the spot as if he could see the actual victim.

"Are you comparing it to the crime-scene photos we took?" Keira asked.

"Yes." His gaze left the sand and traveled up the cliff face.

"If she'd fallen over in almost any other spot she might have been stopped by some of these outcroppings, although that probably wouldn't have saved her life."

"The rock she was hit with is what killed her, right?"

"According to the medical examiner."

Folding her arms across her body Keira shivered. While she'd been hiking, the physical activity had warmed her. Now that they'd stopped, however, she was beginning to feel a distinct chill. Whether it was due to the increasing wind off the ocean or to being at the scene of such a senseless crime wasn't clear. One particular thought that had occurred to her before, however, suddenly seemed crucial.

"You know," Keira ventured, "it would be really dumb for a killer to push somebody off a cliff right in his own back-yard. I mean, think about it. Charles lives in the old light-house keeper's quarters right up there. Why in the world would he throw anyone off *this* cliff? That's crazy."

"Good question. I didn't peg him as the impulsive type. Of course, anything can happen in a moment of rage."

"Except that Charles and Olivia got along. Nobody ever saw them fight or even disagree."

"She could be moody, though. I read that in the transcripts of the original interviews."

Keira had to smile. "She was a woman. We're all moody at times. Ask any man. Start with my brothers. They'll tell you plenty about Fiona and me."

She was glad to see Nick's head nod and his shoulders shake in a silent laugh. He had his back to her and was hunkered down, probing in the sand at the base of the cliff, while she stood back and observed.

A particularly noisy group of gulls launched themselves from the promontory directly above, causing Keira to glance their way.

What she saw stole her breath. She gasped. Tried to

scream loud enough to be heard over the noise of the surf and screeching seabirds.

Nick didn't acknowledge her warning. There wasn't time for another. A boulder was teetering directly over him, ready to crash down onto the beach. Perhaps to kill him in virtually the same spot where Olivia had died!

Keira could not let that happen. She had to do something. Anything. Now!

Launching herself like an Olympic runner coming off the starting blocks, she raced toward him.

Fist-size rocks and whitish, irregular clumps of dirty snow were already falling. The hardest projectiles were bouncing off larger outcroppings and chipping fragments loose, while the softer snow was scattered and fell as cascades of slush.

Nick raised his arms to shield himself, not realizing that the initially light shower of dirt, pebbles and snow was about to become life-threatening.

Keira could tell there wasn't time to pull him out of the way. Shadows of the coming avalanche darkened her path, making her wonder if she was going to be too late. If she was going to die with her partner.

Noticing her rapid approach, Nick started to rise.

She hit him squarely in the chest, her hands out, arms extended, and they both crashed back against the undercut base of the cliff.

For a moment after the boulder came to rest, there was a further shower of pebbles. Then, even the gulls fell silent.

Keira was afraid to move. Afraid to let herself make a personal assessment, let alone speak. Seconds passed like hours. The world spun in slow motion.

"Are—are you all right?" she finally managed to say, barely able to form the words because there didn't seem to be adequate air to breathe.

Nick's voice rumbled, "I think so."

He had both arms wrapped around her tightly and didn't seem ready to let go, which was just fine with Keira. Chances were good she wouldn't be able to function normally for a few minutes, anyway. She was trembling too badly.

Beginning to stroke her back through her jacket, Nick said, "That was close. Did you see what happened?"

"Only that there was a rock about to flatten you."

"Why didn't you just yell for me to get out of the way?"

Apparently she had lost her FBPD cap during her mad dash because she could feel his chin pressed against the top of her head and his breath whispering through her hair.

Keira had anticipated his question, she just hadn't expected him to ask it with such tenderness and not a glimmer of anger.

"I did. You didn't hear me." She laid her cheek against his chest and listened to both their hearts' runaway cadence. "I didn't know what else to do."

"You risked your life," Nick said quietly.

"You're my partner," Keira told him. "That's what partners do."

Waiting for his rebuttal she was shocked to receive a stronger, tighter hug, instead. She wasn't the only one shaking like a leaf in the aftermath of their close call, she realized. Nick Delfino, the big, strong city cop who wasn't afraid of anything, was trembling as much as she was. Maybe more.

Nick didn't know how many minutes they'd sat there, embracing and catching their breath. The way he saw it, as long as they were tucked in against the recess at the base of the cliff, they'd be safer than if they ventured out or showed themselves too soon.

Besides, he added silently, he wanted to be certain his knees would support him when he finally did decide to get up.

The whole momentary scenario kept repeating in his mind's eye. Keira diving for him. That boulder just missing her. Them. *Dear God.* If he were a praying man...

She placed a palm against his chest and began to exert gentle pressure. "We'd better report in."

"Right."

He was going to have to let go of her and admit to himself how much he hated doing so. Keira would never suspect that unacceptable weakness in his character, of course. It was just that he knew how close she'd come to sacrificing her life for his and that knowledge had hit him like a sucker punch.

He kept one hand on her arm as she eased herself away. "Don't stick your head out yet," Nick cautioned. "Sit tight till we get some backup."

Judging by Keira's expression of disbelief and shock, he was certain she had assumed the landslide was accidental.

"You—you don't think...?"

"I don't know. When you notify the station, don't scare anybody unnecessarily. Just keep in mind what you said when we were walking over here."

Keira paused with her radio in hand. "W-what? What did I say?"

"That this area of the bay had stayed virtually the same for years. Oh, sure, a few small rocks might fall from time to time, but when was the last time you saw an avalanche like this without being able to blame a bad storm or new erosion for causing it?"

"Never," she whispered.

"That's my point. I can't imagine how anyone could have purposely dislodged a rock that big without their suspicious activity being noticed, but we have to assume this was no accident until we've had a chance to prove otherwise. Understand?"

"Yes."

She stayed close to him and seated herself on the damp sand. After three failed attempts to radio the station, she said, "I guess I need to be farther from the cliff. The signal isn't getting through."

"Then we'll both go. Together," Nick said. He stood and offered his hand, no longer worried about whether she might misunderstand. This woman had literally saved his life. The least he could do was help her up.

Keira accepted his gallantry without question. Her fingers felt chilly within his and he wanted to once more wrap his arms around her and offer warmth, support, additional thanks.

Instead, he settled for slipping one arm across her shoulders and holding her motionless until he'd made sure that there was nothing unusual occurring on the cliff edge. The seabirds had gone back to their normal activities, too. Another good sign.

"All right," Nick said. "When I count to three, we'll make a run for that open place on the beach over there. See where I'm pointing?"

Her nod satisfied him. She was shivering as if they'd just been doused in ice water, even though only parts of their uniforms had gotten damp from the sand.

Nick tightened his grip on her shoulder. "One, two, three. Go!"

She stumbled several times but his support was enough to keep either of them from falling. As soon as they were in the clear, he could see far enough over the lip of the precipice and tell that there was no one lurking up there. So far, so good.

"Okay. Call it in. And be sure to tell them not to drive too close to the edge if they approach from the top. We want to preserve possible clues."

"Right."

While Keira reported their position and situation, Nick stayed right next to her. Yes, they were safe now. And no, there was no good reason for him to continue to be so defensive. He didn't care. He wasn't leaving his partner's side until he was ordered to. And maybe not even then.

"They want us to start walking back because of the incoming tide," Keira told Nick. She knew he'd been listening to her radio conversation but she felt she must say something.

"I suppose we have no choice. I wouldn't want to scale that cliff even if it was stable."

"You think the landslide may have been an accident, then?" she asked, holding her breath in the hope he wasn't convinced that they'd been attacked again.

Nick arched a brow and gave her a look that said more than his verbal reply. "What do you think?"

"I think I'm getting awfully sick of feeling like a target," Keira said honestly. "If that was the only thing that had happened to us lately, I might be willing to give it the benefit of the doubt. Under the circumstances, I have to say I think it was done on purpose. What I can't figure out is *how*. Or *why*."

"I take it you don't think God is mad at you and wanted to get your attention."

Keira had to laugh. "Nope." She cast her partner a lopsided grin. "Of course I can't speak for *you*, Delfino."

"I think God prefers to just ignore me," Nick countered, returning her wry smile. "If you're ready, then let's get started back."

She considered insisting that she could make the hike without touching him but the feel of his hand holding hers was just too wonderful to forgo. True, their embrace after the near miss may have been a bit excessive, but there was really nothing wrong with walking hand in hand. For the sake of safety and speed, naturally.

Yeah, right, her conscience argued. Keira knew better than that. She was letting this man touch her because that was what she wanted him to do, not because it was necessary or even wise. And she'd be delighted if he continued to hold her hand indefinitely.

That would certainly please Aunt Vanessa, Keira thought, blushing as she realized she was giving this incident far too much importance. Nick was simply being chivalrous toward her, not romantic. How silly to imagine otherwise.

Thoughts spinning out of control, Keira decided to mention something that had been on her mind of late. All Nick could do was refuse her invitation. Yes, it would hurt her feelings if he did, but it wasn't the end of the world. Besides, if she asked him while he was still in such a receptive mood, the chances of his acceptance were greater.

Before she could change her mind she blurted it out. "There's a Valentine's Day party coming up at the Sugar Plum Café. Their first annual Chocolate Extravaganza."

"I think I noticed a poster for it when I was staying at the inn."

"Oh. Good."

Keeping her eyes on the sand and her head turned away so Nick couldn't see how much she was blushing, she tried to make her invitation sound nonchalant. Unfortunately, her explanation came out distorted when she said, "It would be just like going to the funeral."

Nick laughed. "Huh?"

"I meant you could watch people there." *Oh, dear.* No wonder guys had so much trouble asking women for dates. This wasn't easy.

"Are you trying to say you'd like me to go to the party with you?" Nick asked, still laughing softly.

"If you think it would be all right, yes. I don't want you to feel pressured or anything. I just thought it would be another chance for you to meet people casually and size them up without having to use your badge to ask questions."

"Right. It's just business. I get it."

To Keira's chagrin he released her hand, though he did stay close as they trudged back up the shoreline. That invitation had certainly not come out the way she'd meant it to. Still, since Nick had agreed to accompany her, there was hope he hadn't taken offense.

What more can I ask for? Keira thought. *We hardly know each other. If we hadn't faced danger together—more than once—chances are we'd be no more than friendly acquaintances. Or even less.*

But they had come through the fire together, so to speak, and it had led them to a surprisingly rapid sense of closeness. At least, it had in Keira's case. She couldn't help feeling as if she and Nick had been partners for ages and had developed their camaraderie over the course of time. It was as if their relationship had been running like a film on fast-forward. Unclear, yet moving quickly.

"Fine. I'll pick up the tickets tomorrow," she said, chancing a peek over at him when he didn't object. "No arguments?"

"Nope. I'm good."

Although her quick wit kept insisting she answer with a flippant comment regarding his obvious goodness, she restrained herself. It was bad enough that he thought she was only asking him to the party for business reasons. Joking about it would make things worse.

If that's even possible, Keira mused, disgusted. Nick was evidently convinced that her only interest in him was because of their shared goal of solving the murder. How

could she soften that opinion and convince him she had no
ulterior motives? More importantly, how was she going to
convince *herself*?

NINE

They reached the rear of the old mill. Nick stepped into the basement, turned and offered his hand.

When Keira grasped it, he suspected she held on for longer than was necessary. That wouldn't have been so bad if her brother Douglas hadn't seen everything as he jogged across the basement, shoved past Nick and gathered her into his arms.

"You okay?"

"Of course," Keira assured him. "We both are."

"You'd better be," the captain warned with an angry expression directed pointedly at Nick. "Come with me. I'll drive. There's something I want you to see."

Following, Nick climbed into the back of Douglas's cruiser while Keira rode shotgun in the front seat. She'd shocked him when she'd asked him out, even if her motives hadn't been as sociable as he'd first thought. Nevertheless, it was a perfect opportunity for him to do a little casual sleuthing. Couldn't complain about that.

He caught the captain glaring at him in the rearview mirror as if he had somehow been responsible for the near accident beneath the cliff. Nick figured, under the circumstances, saying nothing was wiser than trying to make excuses.

Keira's family was probably going to blame him no matter what he said.

A metal grill separated prisoners from the officers in the front of the car. Nick leaned forward and gripped the grid with his fingertips. "I can understand why our collars don't like riding back here. It's intimidating."

"You're just lucky you don't have to share the space with a snarling police dog," Douglas said curtly. "Be thankful the department doesn't own one."

The captain finally wheeled into the drive leading to the grounds of the lighthouse. Charles's red-roofed home sat off to one side and there were no vehicles in the parking lot except black-and-whites.

"Is this every patrol car you own?" Nick asked.

"All but the SUV Keira's been driving." The captain had to release Nick from the outside. "Watch where you walk. We have some tire tracks we're looking at near the edge."

Nick fell into step behind the others. Douglas's resolve was evident, leading Nick to conclude that whatever they'd found must be telling.

Since Keira, too, was walking ahead of him it was easy for Nick to observe her. That's why, when she rounded the front police car and pulled up short with an audible gasp, he was fully aware of her reaction.

Leaning past her shoulder he saw snow and underlying sod that had been shoved up into ridges like a crumpled throw rug. The path of the disturbance led straight to the cliff. So did the tire tracks.

"Somebody pushed that stuff down on us," Nick said softly.

Keira nodded. "See where it came from? There are dozens of natural boulders used as barricades around the parking lot so nobody can accidentally drive over the cliff. One of them is missing. Somebody had to push it a long way in order to try to drop it on us."

"How would they know we were down there?" Nick asked. "I doubt you can see the beach without hanging over the edge of the cliff."

"You can if you look from that direction," Douglas volunteered, pointing north toward an irregularity in the promontory. "What I don't get is why all this is happening. Except for the one murder, we had practically no violence in Fitzgerald Bay until *you* were transferred here, Delfino."

"That's not fair," Keira piped up. "You're forgetting the problem with the gang member who was chasing Merry and little Tyler."

"I'm not forgetting anything. That crime is solved," her brother insisted. "Merry is adopting Tyler and his birth father will be cooling his heels in jail till the kid is old enough to be out of college. What I'd like to know is who has it in for Delfino, here."

"Maybe it's somebody who doesn't want me to solve the Henry murder," Nick said. "Have you considered that?"

The captain nodded. "Yes, we have." He paused to eye his sister as if trying to read her mind. "How about it, Keira? Do you have any idea what's going on?"

She shook her head. "Not a clue."

Nick remained silent. He had an idea all right. The only factor that didn't fit was Keira's presence when the boulder had fallen. He wouldn't put it past Olivia Henry's killer to use violence to try to stop his investigation but he couldn't imagine the Fitzgeralds taking a chance on injuring a member of their family in the process. Maybe they hadn't know that Keira was down there with him.

He had almost convinced himself that the allegations against this little police department were false until this most recent attack. Now, he was far less confident.

Taking slow, cautious steps, Nick edged closer to the precipice so he could make personal observations. Whoever had done this must have been driving a pretty heavy vehicle with a high bumper.

He sensed Keira at his elbow, crouched and pointed to the tread marks imprinted in the sod. "Looks like a truck."

"Uh-huh. Our old friends, maybe?"

"Could be. I don't suppose there's a traffic cam or any other such device around here."

"In Fitzgerald Bay? We don't even have a camera over the bank's outdoor ATM."

"That figures."

"You'd think somebody would have noticed a truck pushing a big rock around," she said. "I mean, think about it. How odd is it to see a guy shoving boulders off the cliff?"

"Unless..." Nick straightened and scanned the area, deciding that no matter how far-fetched his idea might be, it was worth looking into.

He cupped Keira's elbow and hurried her back to where the captain was conversing with other officers.

"Excuse me," Nick said. "I was wondering. I've never seen snowplows working around town but I know you must have them. If I were you, I'd check their tires for a match and dust the cabs for prints." He could tell by the way Keira was grinning that she thought he was onto something. Now all he had to do was convince her brother.

That wasn't as difficult as Nick had feared. Muttering under his breath for a moment, Douglas gave the necessary orders and the others quickly dispersed.

Then he turned to Nick. "Good call, Delfino. Nobody would pay the slightest attention to a truck with a blade pushing piles of snow around this time of year. Most of our units have dual axles but there is one that could have left these tracks. It's small enough to work in tight spaces and still have the power to do this."

"Hey!" Keira was beaming at her partner. "They said you were really smart. I'm beginning to think they didn't give you nearly enough credit."

"Thanks. Just trying to think outside the box."

His gaze softened as he saw the admiration blossoming in her expression. She seemed to be developing a gigantic case of hero worship and there wasn't a thing he could do to stop it.

It would end with a bang, of course. Once he revealed his true mission at the FBPD, Keira would hate him. He didn't blame her. Didn't really blame any of the officers and departments he was assigned to investigate. Somebody had to act as the conscience of law enforcement and Nick figured it may as well be him. At least he was unbiased and would turn in an accurate assessment.

Even this time? Yes. Especially this time. Because if he failed to uncover the killer it would look even worse for the chief and all the other Fitzgeralds.

Why should I care? Nick asked himself.

The answer to that was easy. She was standing right there in front of him, looking at him as if he were the quintessential cop. He knew better. In those fleeting moments when he had seen Keira nearly perish, his first reaction had not been to perform beyond human capabilities.

It had been spiritual. He'd thanked God. The God he'd insisted he didn't believe in.

Keira felt short of breath every time she thought of how close she and Nick had come to being crushed to death. Replaying the incident over and over in her mind did little to comfort her, either. The more she visualized it, the more she realized how crazy she had been to run into the path of such imminent danger.

Lagging back while Nick talked to some of the other officers and watched them making imprints of the tire tracks leading to the cliff, she leaned against the side of one of the black-and-whites. She was still standing like that when Charles drove up with his two-year-old twins.

Instead of setting them on their feet after he freed them from their car seats, he gathered one in each arm and headed straight for Keira.

She greeted him with a wan smile. "You missed all the fun."

"Looks like it. What happened? Not another killing, I hope."

"No. But it was a close call."

"What?"

His alarmed expression spurred her to quickly explain. "Everybody's fine. Nick and I were down on the beach when somebody shoved a boulder off the cliff. It just missed us. Talk about scary."

"You're all right? You're sure?"

"I'm fine. A little wobbly. Just don't tell Nick or the others. I think I've convinced them I'm a lot tougher than I really am."

"Would you like to come inside and unwind? We can talk after I find the kids something to keep them occupied."

Although Keira smiled she also shook her head. "I should stay out here. It's my job."

"What does Dad have to say about that?"

"Please." She rolled her eyes. "I have enough trouble convincing people I'm a real cop. The last thing I need is to have everybody see my father overprotecting me."

"He cares about your safety. We all do."

"I know. The trouble is, I want to stand on my own two

feet and that's pretty hard to do around here." The moment she spoke she saw Charles assessing her posture, clearly noting the fact she was still leaning against the car.

Abashed, she pushed away, straightened and laughed softly. "Okay, so maybe I am a little overwhelmed right now. That has to be normal. Even Nick was shaking after it happened—and he's an old pro."

"Delfino was with you?"

"Yes, of course. I was showing him where..." Keira eyed the twins, then chose not to finish her sentence.

"Okay. Who knew you were headed down there?"

"I'd notified the station."

"Plus half the town if you used your radio," Charles added. "You know how many people own scanners so they can listen to fire and police chatter."

"That's right."

She jumped when a voice close behind her asked, "What is?"

Whirling, she tried to hide her nervousness from Nick. "Hi. I didn't hear you coming. Are they finished making imprints of the tire tracks?"

"Yeah." He put out his palm to shake hands with Charles before smiling and withdrawing the offer. "Sorry. I see you have your hands full. Good to see you, doc. What have you been up to?"

"You mean, do I have an alibi for this afternoon? Yes, I do. We were paying a call on my grandfather Ian. He likes to visit with the twins when there's not as much distraction as there is when we have our monthly family get-togethers."

"Sounds like that might be a little hectic," Nick said, still smiling and eyeing Keira. "But if my partner was to ask me to join her the next time, I might agree to tough it out."

Keira was astounded. And speechless. She cast a pleading glance at Charles, hoping he'd come up with a suitable, polite excuse for not taking Nick seriously. Unfortunately, her brother appeared to be as shocked as she was.

Nick chuckled. "Hey, don't let it bother you. I know it's a family thing. I just thought, since she'd already asked me to the Valentine's party, she might like to include me in something a little more casual."

The wide-eyed look on Charles's face might have made Keira laugh if she weren't so uptight. "I—I…"

Her brother found his voice before she did and what he said floored her.

"I see no reason why you shouldn't come to dinner," Charles said flatly. "Once you've met the rest of the Fitzgerald clan you'll be less likely to distrust us." He cleared his throat. "We'll all be at Dad's this coming Saturday night. If you're interested in joining us, be there before six-thirty."

When Nick said, "Thanks. I'd love to come," Keira almost gasped. It was one thing to put up with her partner's no-nonsense attitude at work. That she could manage. But the idea of what would happen once he was surrounded by her boisterous, eclectic family gave her gooseflesh and made her heart pound.

At that moment she wasn't sure whether she was more worried about what Nick would say and do, or about how her relatives might treat him. If they thought he was being antagonistic they might turn on him en masse. If that happened, Nick would find out firsthand what it was like to be a part of a close-knit family group—only his place would be on the outside looking in.

By the time they got through with Nick, she'd be fortunate if he was still coherent, let alone willing to attend the Valentine's bash with her as he'd promised.

In a way, she was glad he'd have a taste of her family dynamics before they went out on what she considered the equivalent of a date. Yes, he had misunderstood the true motives behind her invitation. That had been her fault for trying to minimize her desire to go out with him.

But that didn't change the fact that she had asked and he had accepted. All she could hope for was that Nick wouldn't find her clan too intimidating or be put off by their personal questions. Aunt Vanessa wasn't the only Fitzgerald who tended to play matchmaker, even if she was the most outspoken.

Keira managed a smile for Nick as Charles bid them goodbye and walked away. "You really don't have to feel obligated to come to dinner at Dad's. I know you prefer solitude and you sure won't find it at a Fitzgerald gathering."

"Not a problem," Nick said, grinning. "I wouldn't miss it for the world."

TEN

Keira was surprised when her father called her into his office the following afternoon. She knew she'd been walking a proverbial tightrope since she'd been partnered with Nick but as far as she could tell, she hadn't gotten into trouble, with or without him, for at least the past twenty-four hours.

She poked her head through the doorway without fully entering. "You wanted to see me, Chief?"

"Yes. Come in. Close the door."

Uh-oh. "Is there a problem?"

"I don't know. You tell me."

Puzzled, she plunked down in a leather chair opposite her father and studied his expression. "Tell you what?"

"About your partner, for starters. What have you learned about him?"

"You have his personnel file. I'm sure you know more than I do. Why?"

Aiden shook his head. "I'm not talking about what's in the man's file. I want your personal opinion of him."

The color started to flood Keira's cheeks. She squirmed, straightened in the chair and cleared her throat. "My personal opinion? In what way?"

"Do you think he's honest?"

"Of course I do." Scowling, she leaned forward and stared

at her father, trying to figure out his strange mood. "You're the one who agreed to bring him here in the first place and you said he had good credentials. Why would you ask me something like that?"

Aiden shoved a sheet of paper across the desk toward her.

She picked it up and scanned it. "I don't understand. This says we got a hit on fingerprints from the only snowplow that matched the tire tracks on scene at the cliff. So?"

"Keep reading."

"Okay, being in the FBI's Integrated Automated Fingerprint Identification System database means this Anthony Carlton is a known criminal. IAFIS should be able to provide a mug shot."

"I got one all right. Check those details again."

Turning back to the report she read, then reread, before looking up. "I think I see what you mean. What do you want me to do about it?"

"Nothing, for the present," Aiden said, passing her a photo of a middle-aged, slightly portly man with light, receding hair and a mustache. The picture looked like an official ID. The subject was wearing a police uniform.

"Just keep working with Delfino and keep your ears open," Aiden said. "And please be careful. Until we can fill in the blanks, we won't know enough to tell if Carlton's the underlying reason for the recent rash of incidents."

"But you think he may be? That's ridiculous."

"Maybe. Maybe not. I'm keeping an open mind. The prints prove that the guy who pushed that boulder off the cliff was a former lieutenant on the same Boston department as Nick. That's too much of a coincidence to suit me. Unfortunately, portions of Carlton's record have been sealed by a judge. It'll take time to get access. Until we do, I don't want Delfino to know about the hit on the prints."

Keira was astounded. She saw no alternative so she agreed. "All right. I won't breathe a word until I clear it with you."

She rose, handed back the report and the photo to her father, and chanced a smile. "Speaking of Nick reminds me. I meant to mention it earlier. Charles invited him to dinner Saturday tonight."

"What? That's when we're getting together with family at my place."

"Exactly," Keira said, starting to inch toward the door and put more distance between herself and her father. "Nick will be joining all of us at the house tomorrow evening. I made sure to tell Irene so she'd prepare enough food."

"And when were you planning to tell *me?*"

"I just did." She gave him a mock salute, hoping it would soften his mood, and was relieved to see him shake his head the way he did when capitulating.

"Okay. I guess that'll work to our advantage. I'll inform your other brothers and we can all keep an eye on him, see if we can draw him out about his past."

"I hope you have better luck than I've had," Keira said. She paused with her hand on the doorknob. "Nick and I have been together since the day after he hit town and I still don't know much about him except that his parents are retired and living in Florida. I think the size of our family intimidates him."

"Good," Aiden said. "I want him on edge. If he's involved with a crooked cop and thinks he can hide out in *my* town, he's got another think coming."

"Now you sound like the folks who were ready to lynch Charles the moment Olivia's body was discovered. That's not like you, Dad."

"This has nothing to do with Olivia Henry." Aiden was suddenly all business again. "I wouldn't have agreed to bring in an outsider if it wasn't for the sake of your brother. Now I suspect I made a mistake."

"If you did, it was only because you love us all," Keira told him. "We'll solve the murder. I know we will. And if Nick is as clever about those clues as he was when he thought of checking the snowplow, maybe it won't take too long."

As she turned and left the office she heard her father say, "I hope you're right."

Nick had tried again to contact his former boss, had failed to connect privately and had left a message asking for a return call ASAP. It didn't come. That apparent lack of commitment to his current mission was very troubling.

It was almost as if he were the one being ostracized instead of the crooked former lieutenant he'd accused of accepting huge bribes to "lose" evidence and thereby protect members of a crime syndicate. The proof against that officer and several others had been irrefutable, yet before all the warrants could be served the chief suspect had vanished.

Nick knew there was no way Anthony Carlton or his cohorts could have known they were about to be arrested unless someone on the inside had tipped them off. Someone who was undoubtedly still on the force. Was that why Nick's calls weren't being returned? Was someone in Boston purposely misdirecting the messages to keep him in the dark? Was Carlton still at large?

Even if that was so, it didn't change anything. He had a job to do and he'd do it whether he received outside assistance or not. There had been times in the past when he'd likened his position to that of a soldier caught behind enemy lines. This assignment was no different. Operating on his own often provided the best results, anyway.

He showered and shaved, then donned slacks and the green sweater he'd worn before. Except for his uniforms and other duty gear, he hadn't brought much with him. Socializing wasn't his forte. He much preferred the predictable public image of an officer of the law to the unknowns he might face if he were forced to step out of character.

Why was that? he wondered. He could hold his own in conversations about myriad subjects and his manners were impeccable, thanks to his rigid upbringing. Still, he was happiest playing the role of a cop. It was his identity. His destiny.

A knocking startled him. "Yes?"

"It's me. Your landlord," Douglas Fitzgerald called. "Since you don't have your own car I thought you might want to hitch a ride with me to Dad's party."

Nick's gut was in a knot when he opened the door. "Party? I thought this was just a family dinner."

"It is. We meet once a month for a good meal and to celebrate any birthdays."

"I don't need to bring presents, do I?" Nick scanned the sparse apartment behind him as if doing so might provide needed gifts right out of the blue.

The captain patted him on the shoulder. "Nah. You're good. We sometimes give gag gifts but to tell you the truth, I'm not sure any of the clan have February birthdays. I know my siblings and I don't." He grinned. "Relax, man. We won't bite."

His comment made Nick chuckle. "That's a relief. I was figuring you all would eat me alive."

"Only if we thought you were being unfair to our baby sister or putting her in danger," Douglas said, still smiling although not as broadly as before.

"She's really amazing," Nick told him. "When I first saw her I had no idea."

"Her apparent naïveté may be Keira's most valuable asset on the streets. Crooks will underestimate her. Her biggest problem is her self-confidence."

"She has plenty of that," Nick said, pulling on a coat and following Douglas outside.

"I know. I meant she has way too much trust in her own abilities. Someday that's going to get her into trouble and there's not a thing any of us can do to keep it from happening."

"Oh, I don't know." Nick climbed into the dark blue SUV in the driveway and slammed the door, continuing their conversation as soon as Douglas slid behind the wheel. "I think she's getting more savvy. At least, that's how it seems to me."

"Good. We had hoped that would be the result of assigning her to work with somebody she didn't know."

Nick noticed the other man eyeing him while driving. "Glad to be of service."

"Yeah, well, try to keep her farther from trouble than you have so far. I'd just as soon she didn't get hurt while you're teaching her how to be a good cop."

Hurt? "Sometimes that kind of thing is inevitable," Nick said quietly, contemplating what would happen once Keira learned of his undercover assignment. Hopefully, by that time, she'd be seasoned enough to realize that he'd just been following orders and that he, personally, had not intended to harm her or any other member of her family.

They pulled to a stop in front of an immense white New England Colonial–style home.

"Nice little place your father has here."

"We needed every inch of it when all six of us were growing up. Now it's just Keira and Dad. He has a live-in housekeeper, too. Irene Mulrooney."

"I saw her at the memorial service with Charles and his kids. Older woman, gray hair?"

"That's her. Just don't let her hear you call her 'older,'" Douglas warned with a muted chuckle.

"Noted."

"Irene's a treasure. She likes to mother all of us, even now that we're adults. After our mother passed away, it was Irene who held the family together. She's a truly good woman."

"And a great cook, according to Keira," Nick said. He got out, surprised that Douglas didn't follow. "Aren't you coming in?"

"I have to go pick up someone else," the captain said, coloring slightly and leaning across the front seat to speak to Nick. "I imagine my gabby sister has told you all about me and Merry O'Leary."

"She may have mentioned it."

"I'm sure she did. Just go on in. Keira's waiting for you."

"Right. Thanks for the ride."

Steeling himself, Nick approached the front door, paused to stomp bits of clinging snow off his shoes and wiped the soles on a mat.

Well, here goes nothing, he thought, taking a deep breath and steeling himself for the coming ordeal. He'd rather face an armed criminal than spend the evening pretending to befriend unsuspecting folks who were welcoming him into their home as if he belonged.

As far back as he could remember, Nick had always felt like an outsider, even when he was with people he'd known for years. Nothing had changed since then. He was still on the outside looking in and probably always would be. That wasn't a condemnation; it was a simple fact.

Long before this assignment, before he'd even entered the police academy, he'd failed to fit in. Perhaps that was one thing that made him a good cop. He hoped so.

He also hoped he could pull off this charade and convince the Fitzgeralds he was just a regular guy. It was going to take an Academy Award performance to do so but he was up to it. If he could infiltrate a gang of crooked cops and bust their operation wide open, he could certainly manage to come off as a normal person.

That thought made him smile in spite of his nervousness. *Normal* was not an adjective that had ever applied to him. Not as a child or youth, and certainly not at present.

It was also not a condition to which he aspired, Nick assured himself. He was happy being the outsider. The misfit. The malcontent. Because while he stood apart from the complicated relationships of others, he could not possibly be hurt.

A shrink would have a field day with that one, he mused, feeling cynical, *but it's the truth.*

Nick Delfino was one of those people who had never belonged. Not really. Not in his deepest heart. And those others who claimed kinship to anyone or anything were as foreign to him as if they'd just beamed to earth from an alien spaceship.

He raised his arm, grabbed the brass knocker and let it fall.

Keira had spent the time primping in the hall mirror since she'd heard her brother's SUV pull up in front. She gave one last tug on the hem of her blue cashmere sweater and smoothed it over the hips of her jeans.

When she heard Nick's knock she already had her hand on the knob. She jerked open the door. There he stood, smiling and looking surprised by her instantaneous response.

Keira was so delighted she immediately set aside any misgivings about his past in Boston and welcomed him. Fortunately, she retained enough self-control to temper her grin, shake his hand and use it to pull him inside. "I'm glad you decided to join us." She peered past his broad shoulders. "Isn't Douglas coming in?"

"He said he was going to get someone else."

"Ah, of course. Merry and her little boy. Can I take your coat?" While he removed it she watched him scan the foyer. "This is quite a place."

"I've never lived anywhere else," Keira said. "Every time I mention getting a home of my own, Dad looks so sad I back off. I suppose I'll have to leave the nest someday. I just hate to think of him here in this big old house all by himself."

"I thought the housekeeper lived here, too."

"She does, but I'm the baby of the Fitzgerald kids." Keira took Nick's jacket and hung it in the hall closet. "Everybody else is gathering in the dining room. Come on. I'll introduce you to the ones you don't already know from work."

"From the sound of it, half the town must be here."

"Not quite. My aunt Vanessa and uncle Joe had to work. Fiona and her son, Sean, are here, though. And Douglas will want you to meet Merry and Tyler when they arrive. He's definitely serious about her. Like I said before, Aunt Vanessa claims credit for that, although I think the real matchmaker was the good Lord."

She took Nick's arm to urge him along when she noticed that his steps weren't matching hers, then guided him down the wide hall, past the staircase leading to the second story and toward the formal dining room. Irene had set the table with a pristine white linen cloth, put out the company china and stemware, and had added a centerpiece of fresh-cut flowers.

Conversation that had been loud and animated suddenly ceased. All eyes turned toward the doorway where Keira and Nick stood.

Grinning broadly, Keira proudly announced, "For those of you who don't already know, this is my new partner, Nick Delfino. He's going to be joining us for dinner tonight."

When no one moved forward to shake Nick's hand and welcome him, Keira was taken aback. Surely they couldn't all share her father's concern that Nick might be guilty of being involved with the fugitive Boston cop. Placing blame like that was so unfair. And, hopefully, totally wrong.

Keira refused to accept the somber disposition of the group. "I've been telling Nick what a great family I have. Now show him or you'll make me look bad."

Stately, gray-haired octogenarian Ian Fitzgerald was the first to smile and step forward to offer his hand. "Pleased to meet you, Nick. What do you think of our little town?"

Nick shook the still-spry elderly gentleman's hand and mirrored his amiability. "What I've seen of it so far is very impressive, sir."

Glad to hear her grandfather chuckle as a result of Nick's reply, Keira grinned and explained, "Granddad was chief of police before my father so he knows all about what's been happening."

"In that case I suppose I should admit that being here has already shaved years off my life," Nick added with a wry grin. "It's certainly not dull."

Stepping forward to join them, her brother Ryan offered his hand. "Nick's renting a condo from Douglas so we'd better humor him. Good to see you away from the office, Delfino."

"Likewise."

That exchange and handshake was enough to loosen up everyone else and the background conversation resumed.

Keira took Nick's arm and guided him through the room while making further introductions. "This is my sister, Fiona Cobb. And that darling six-year-old pushing the toy fire truck around under the table is her son, Sean."

Fiona grasped Nick's hand and smiled. "Pleased to finally meet you, Nick. Keira's told me a lot about you."

"All good, I hope."

While Keira held her breath, her sister giggled and replied, "For the most part. You'll have to make time to visit my bookstore soon and we can talk more."

"I'd like that."

"He'll probably end up trying to pump you for information about the murder," Keira added aside. "I hope you won't take offense. Nick can be kind of single-minded at times."

"No more than my Jimmy was," Fiona said wistfully. "I wish you'd met him, Nick. He'd help you adjust to this crazy family of ours."

"Do I look maladjusted?" Nick quipped.

That made Keira laugh aloud. "You look terrified, if you must know. I was afraid you were going to bolt and make a run for it when you first saw all of us in one place."

"And this isn't all, as you well know," Fiona added. "Just think of us as a winning football team and a pack of crazy cheerleaders."

"I'll try. I can't wait to see you form one of those cheerleader pyramids." He smiled but was scanning the room. "This ceiling is almost high enough for one."

"Hey, it takes a big house to hold us all. You should see this place when everybody in the family shows up."

"I can hardly wait."

Nick's expression reflected the opposite in spite of his obvious efforts to appear at ease. It amused Keira to see that his wangling of an invitation had backfired on him.

Leaving Fiona, Keira made sure Nick shook hands with her brother Owen, whom he knew from the station, of course, and her uncle Mickey and his wife, Jenny, before directing him to where Charles was sitting on the floor, stacking wooden blocks so his twin two-year-olds could gleefully knock them down.

The doctor got to his feet, smiled and offered his hand. "I see you made it, Nick. Have you gotten any word on the new DNA test yet?"

Nick shook his head. "No. Sorry. The lab is always backed up. I've put in a call and asked to be notified immediately but so far I haven't heard a thing."

"It could be months," Keira chimed in. "I wish there was someway to expedite but they don't consider this case a rush job."

Nick agreed. "Right. Because there's no current threat." He smiled at the other man and the children who were now clinging to him, one holding each of his legs below the knees as if they were mimicking old-time firemen about to slide down a brass pole.

"I am glad of that," Charles said with a somber nod. "I'd hate to see anyone else get hurt." As he spoke he laid one hand on the silky black hair of each of his children. "I should have introduced you before. This is Aaron," he said, "and his sister, Brianne."

To Keira's delight, Nick bent and offered his hand to each of the children. Only Aaron accepted. Brianne hid her face against her father's knee.

"Nice policeman?" the boy asked.

"I always try to be nice," Nick replied.

"That's right," Keira told the child. "Police officers like me and your uncles and your grandfather are the good guys. Remember?"

When she glanced at Nick she could tell he was deep in thought because he'd gotten a faraway look in his eyes. Looping her arm through his, she steered him away from the crowd and down the hall toward the kitchen.

"Where are we going?" he asked.

"I figure it's time to give you a little break. I can tell the gang is starting to get to you."

"Am I that transparent?"

"Most of the time, no. Tonight, yes. Don't you have *any*

extended family? Cousins, maybe? Anybody besides your parents?"

"No, and I'm getting more and more thankful by the minute. I don't mean to sound antisocial, Keira, but standing there while everybody sized me up and talked a blue streak was like being nibbled to death by a school of minnows. It wasn't each individual nip that got to me—it was the cumulative effect."

"You need to relax more," she said with a sigh, knowing the Lord was providing the perfect opening for the questions her father had wanted answered. "I can't imagine why you're so tense. Is there something you want to tell me?"

"Like what?"

The inquisitive scowl on Nick's face made him seem even more attractive. Dangerous. Intriguing. That ridiculous reaction made her wonder if she was becoming unbalanced. Suppose her dad was right and this man was a criminal instead of one of the good guys? What then?

She decided to answer Nick's question with one of her own. "For instance, why are you so secretive about your past? I don't care what you did or didn't do while you were growing up. None of us is perfect. It's the future and what you've made of yourself that matters."

"Humph. You think I was a juvenile delinquent?"

"That would explain why you refuse to talk about yourself." One hand came to rest on his arm and she felt solid muscles flinch through the softness of the sweater.

"My record speaks for itself," he said flatly.

"Your record, at least the file Dad was sent, is a joke. It's almost generic."

"Maybe that's because my life is."

"I have trouble buying that," Keira said, speaking gently and keeping hold of his forearm. "But I can wait. I don't want you to feel pressured. You can tell me more when you're ready."

He arched a brow. "What if I never am?"

"Then that will be okay, too." She momentarily tightened her grip before releasing him and smiling. "I know one thing after being your partner, even for such a short time. I know you're a good man. That's enough for me."

The intense emotion that flashed into his expression was gone in a heartbeat, leaving Keira more befuddled than ever.

She wasn't certain, but she could have sworn she'd glimpsed regret. And perhaps a tinge of guilt.

That reaction made her wonder how Nick might be connected to the fugitive who had tried to kill them with that boulder. Was it possible that she had misjudged him?

Her heart said no. Logic wasn't so certain.

ELEVEN

Nick wasn't prepared for the ultramodern kitchen Keira led him into. Judging by the style and age of the rest of the house, he'd expected a much more old-fashioned setup.

Instead, he found track lighting, stainless-steel appliances, granite countertops and cabinets that appeared to be made of oak with stained-glass inserts decorating some of the doors.

He arched his brows. "Wow. This is some layout."

"It's not nearly as impressive as the cook," Keira said. She gestured toward the woman who was standing with her back to them while mashing potatoes.

"Irene!" Keira called. "Look who's here."

The gray-haired housekeeper turned with a smile and wiped her fingers on her apron before offering to shake hands. "This must be Nick. Pleased to meet you. Any friend of Keira's is a friend of mine."

"Thanks." Hiding his discomfiture he looked past her and changed the subject. "Something sure smells good."

"Yankee pot roast. My special recipe. The secret is the thyme," Irene said, beaming. She winked at Keira. "I'm gonna like this one, girl."

Keira's cheeks bloomed, much to Nick's amusement. "Actually, we came out here to escape the crowd in the dining room for a few minutes. Nick's not used to big families and I think we scare him."

"Ha! He doesn't look like the kind who scares easily." She turned to attend to the pot of potatoes. "Tell you what. I'll just scrape these into a big bowl and you two can help me carry everything to the table. How's that?"

"Do I get a taste first?" Nick asked.

Irene raised her brows at him. "There'll be plenty for everybody after Aiden says grace."

Properly chastised, he apologized. "Sorry. I wasn't raised by churchgoers."

"Well," the cook gibed, "as long as you weren't raised in the forest by wolves, as my mother used to say, you'll do fine." She handed him a large, heavy platter. "Put that right in the middle of the table, to one side of the centerpiece."

"Yes, ma'am."

As Nick left the kitchen, Keira leaned close and kissed Irene's rosy cheek. "Thanks for letting us help. I want him to feel at home."

"He's a strange one, he is," Irene said. "Something's eating at him. I can feel it."

"We think so, too, but we're not sure what it is. Dad has some crazy notions but I don't believe the problem can be all that serious. Not for a second."

"Then do like I've always told you and trust your heart. It knows what's best."

"I was kind of hoping you'd be a bit more specific." Keira accepted the bowl of steaming mashed potatoes and prepared to catch up with Nick in the dining room. "I just hope I can tell the difference between my heart and my brain this time, Irene. The longer I'm around Nick, the more confused I seem to be getting."

"Have you prayed about it?"

That question took Keira aback. "I guess not. Not really." She smiled sheepishly. "That would probably be a good idea, huh?"

"It's where I'd start if I wanted to know who to trust. Or who to love."

"Whoa. Who said anything about…" She interrupted herself when she saw Nick coming back. The look she shot at Irene reflected her unspoken thoughts.

"Nobody." Irene displayed a satisfied grin that crinkled the corners of her eyes. "I was just thinkin' out loud." She picked up another bowl and leaned to look past Keira. "Here you go, Nick. Put these carrots anywhere. I like to arrange them on the platter with the roast when I have room but I had to cook too much meat tonight."

"Never too much for me," he said pleasantly.

Keira was pleased to note that his shoulders seemed a little more relaxed and his smile was reaching his eyes. That was a good sign. So was the fact that her family was basically treating him well, although she could tell there was still an undercurrent of mistrust.

When the time finally came that she was allowed to explain about the fingerprint identification, she was certain Nick would understand. After all, he'd suspected Charles of a terrible crime and no one had held a grudge. At least not visibly. Once Nick was cleared of being in cahoots with the Boston criminal, they'd sit down and have a good laugh over the whole misinterpretation. She hoped.

And in the meantime, she planned to take Irene's sage advice and pray about her growing feelings. Yes, Nick was going to leave Fitzgerald Bay as soon as possible. And yes, he was apparently happy living in Boston. But that city wasn't so far away. Certainly not far enough to keep them from seeing each other regularly if that was how their relationship worked out.

Incredulous, Keira bit her lip and shook her head. Here she was, barely acquainted with the poor guy, and she was already imagining them as a couple. How foolish. Yet a very pleasing thought, as well, she added with a tinge of chagrin.

The family was taking their usual seats around the oblong mahogany table as she reentered the dining room, followed by Irene bearing a gravy boat and a basket of steaming rolls.

Keira noted that her usual chair and one next to it had been left empty. That was a relief. She'd feared her father or her brothers might sandwich Nick between them and keep her from running interference. Happily, that was not the case.

Nick placed his burdens on the table, then pulled out a chair for her.

Good manners, she thought. *Another plus.* Now, if she could only keep her family from inundating the man with probing questions, they might all have a chance to enjoy a pleasant evening.

As Nick joined her, Keira folded her hands in her lap and bowed her head with the others. Out of the corner of her eye she saw Nick hesitate, then copy her motions. He was obviously trying to fit in. Too bad he was simply aping them. Oh, well. Perhaps in time he'd change his mind about church. It wasn't likely, she knew, but anything was possible. Especially when God was working in someone's life.

Smiling, she echoed the "Amen" around the table, then reached for the heavy meat platter.

Nick leaned over to help her lift it. Conversation was ongoing and amiable as parents began preparing plates for their youngsters.

The sound of shattering glass startled everyone. The entire crowd froze. Stared at each other. Little ones sensed the adult reaction and whimpered in fright.

Nick didn't hesitate. He swept Keira out of her chair and shoved her under the table.

By the time she asked, "What was that?" her judgment had already eliminated the notion that they'd been shot at. "It sounded like a window breaking."

"Yeah, it did."

"Then let me go. There's no reason for us to hide under here."

"I'll be the judge of that," Nick said gruffly, refusing to release her.

Men were shouting. Aiden's voice rose above the others. "Women and children get down. Charles and Mickey, you're in charge in here while we investigate. Ryan, with me to the front. Owen and Douglas, take the kitchen and check out the back."

Underneath the table, Keira continued to struggle to free herself but Nick refused to release her.

"No. You're staying put," he insisted. "I'd let you go and follow the others in a heartbeat if I thought I could be sure this isn't a repeat of the incident at the beach."

"Don't be ridiculous, Nick. Some idiot probably chucked a rock through the window on a dare, that's all."

"Maybe. Maybe not."

"Well, at least let me see to the other women. I can stand guard over them and the kids while you go do your thing outside."

"Promise that's all you'll do?"

"Yes, yes," Keira vowed. She was growing more irate by the second but she could see Nick's point. And it did make sense to leave someone with the unarmed family members. Someone like her.

Crawling out from beneath the skirt of the linen tablecloth, Keira spotted Charles first. "Is everybody okay?"

"Yes." The doctor had his own children as well as Fiona's

son, Sean, wrapped in a bear hug while Merry clung to Tyler and tried to comfort him. "Not a scratch. You two?"

"We're fine," Nick said. "I'm going to leave Keira with your group. Just keep her here. I'll go see if I can help outside."

"Okay. Go. I'll look after her," Charles said.

It galled Keira—a police officer—to hear herself spoken of in such terms but she wasn't going to argue. The only important thing right now was calming the frightened kids and keeping everybody away from the windows until Nick and the others gave the all clear.

Once that came, she intended to express her displeasure at being relegated to the rear echelon of this battle. Until then, however, she'd protect the innocents just as she'd been told.

It had always amazed her that her father and brothers took their guns with them everywhere. She knew it was department policy to carry, even when off duty; she just hadn't been in a situation where that degree of armament was deemed necessary—until today.

Irene joined the Fitzgerald clan's stragglers in the dining room after several of them had exited through her kitchen at a dead run. She fisted her hands on ample hips. "Well, I never. I fix Aiden's favorite meal and he runs off. What in the world is going on?"

Hurrying to Irene's side, Keira made sure she was safe before she explained. "We'd just started to eat when somebody broke a window."

"Are you all okay?"

"We're fine," Keira said. "I'm sure Dad and the others won't be gone long. Whoever did it is probably miles away by now."

As she spoke, Charles and her uncle Mickey were systematically lowering the blinds so no one standing in the street or driving past could see what was going on in the well-lit room.

"I surely hope so," Irene said. "Do you want me to take the food back to the kitchen and keep it warm?"

"I don't think that will be necessary."

Keira waited until the last blind had been lowered before skirting the table and examining the shattered glass on the floor. A rock the size of half a brick had landed inside, just shy of the window sash, meaning it was probably thrown from some distance away, maybe even as far as the street.

What a sad reflection on Fitzgerald Bay to have both the current mayor, her grandfather, and the police and fire chiefs attacked like this. Well, at least her dad couldn't possibly blame this incident on Nick. No one passing by would have known there was anyone other than her family having dinner there.

The stone was smooth, as if it had come from the shore where waves tumbled rocks together and polished off the rough edges. She nudged it with the toe of her shoe to roll it over, not expecting the other side to look any different.

Her breath caught. What was that black color? It almost looked like... It was! Someone had scrawled one word on the surface with the broad tip of a marking pen.

It said, *LIAR*.

Keira's stomach clenched. This was not a random case of vandalism. Someone outside had purposely targeted the Fitzgeralds. The question was, who had written the cryptic message and which of them was meant to be the recipient?

There were certainly enough choices. Her dad and Uncle Mickey held positions that often resulted in their being unjustly blamed for events beyond their control. And thanks to Burke Hennessy, some deluded folks still insisted on suspecting Charles of Olivia's murder. Plus there was the upcoming mayoral race involving her father.

Don't forget Nick, Keira's thoughts insisted before she summarily dismissed them. Whatever the reason for the one-word accusation, she was positive it couldn't have been aimed at Nick.

She huffed and shook her head as she realized why she was so certain. All the people who might suspect her partner of wrongdoing had been gathered around the dining table. Therefore, unless her father and brothers turned up a suspect in the yard, the incident had to be due to outside forces.

Trying to sound more cheery than she felt, she announced, "Okay, everybody. The blinds are closed and there's no more danger. Let's go back to the table and finish this delicious meal."

Charles agreed. "Good idea. Our private posse is covering the yard so I'm sure there won't be any more trouble." He lifted his children and sat them on their booster seats, then took his place between them. "Let's eat. I'm starved."

"I'll just get the dustpan and sweep up that mess," Irene said.

"Not until I bag that rock for evidence," Keira said.

Keira's glance caught that of her one remaining brother and she saw him nod. He'd seen the clue, too. She was sorry for that because chances were he'd already decided the allegation pointed to him. Unfortunately, she had to agree it was a strong possibility. Which meant there was a fair chance that the Hennessys or their cohorts were responsible. If that were the case, they'd better find a way to prove it without a doubt before saying anything or Burke would start claiming he was being unfairly persecuted.

In small-town affairs there was simply no way to avoid such unjust assumptions. Keira knew that. Nevertheless, what she wanted to do was stand on a soapbox in the town square and proclaim her family's honesty and integrity until the

Hennessys of the world crawled back under the rock they'd come from.

Was that a proper Christian attitude? she asked herself.

Nope. But it was a totally human one.

By the time Nick had gotten outside, the others had dispersed. He'd drawn his gun, pointed it at the night sky and started to work his way around the perimeter of the house.

Nothing. And no one.

He considered calling out, then decided against it. If the Fitzgeralds were as good at their jobs as Keira claimed, they'd make sure of who or what they were shooting at rather than plug him first and then ask questions.

Reaching a corner flanked by a bush with bare branches he readied himself, then whipped around in a firing stance and came face-to-face with Douglas.

Their mutual reactions to the shock of being confronted without firing spoke well of them both.

Nick lowered his weapon and exhaled noisily. "Find anything?"

"No. Nothing. I *want* to suspect it was a kid who broke the window and then took off." He holstered his sidearm.

"Well, if that's the case, at least it was a rock and not a bullet."

"Right. Dad and the others have been all the way around the rest of the house. Let's go back inside."

As Nick put away his gun and fell into step beside his landlord, the other man clapped him on the back. "You're going to think our town is as bad as Boston if this stuff doesn't stop. Any idea who might be stirring up trouble?"

"Me? How would I know?"

"Just wondering. I imagine you made your share of enemies back in Boston, right?"

"I suppose."

"And they might have followed you here?"

Nick shook his head. "That's not likely. I didn't announce where I was going or why. As far as most of the people in my old department are concerned, I'm just taking a few weeks off."

"Any reason for that kind of secrecy?" the captain asked.

"Not really. Why?"

"Curiosity."

Although Nick accepted the terse explanation, it troubled him. There was no way the chief could have learned about his IA work but he supposed they might have tried to look deeper into his background and discovered a few dead ends. He hadn't had much time to cover his tracks when he'd been given this assignment, so there were likely to be some questionable entries in the file he'd dummied up for himself.

As soon as dinner was over and he was alone, he'd try to reach his former chief again and find out more. Until then, all he could do was continue to play his part and hope for the best.

What was the best? That was easy. The best thing, as far as Nick was concerned, would be finding out that the FBPD was clean. Beyond that, solving the murder would be nice but it wasn't critical at this point in time. Once he was able to exonerate the officers who had collected the evidence and questioned townspeople, he'd know the evidence could be trusted and therefore the killer should be easier to pinpoint.

But one thing at a time, he told himself. Right now he had to return to the dinner table and continue to act as if he believed Charles was truly innocent rather than being shielded by his family.

On a gut level that was already a fact. Next, he'd have to prove it. That was likely to be harder than it had seemed at first glance.

A lot harder.

TWELVE

No one had paid much attention to the writing on the rock other than to agree that it should be processed as evidence. In their line of work, idle threats were, unfortunately, all too common.

Keira could tell Nick was getting more restless as the evening dragged on. She figured that if he hadn't had to rely upon someone else to drive him home, he would have excused himself already.

By 9:00 p.m. the children had all dozed off, some in friendly laps, some in the overstuffed furniture of a nearby parlor as the adults sat around and chatted. The twins had conked out first. Tyler was the only one still fighting sleep and he was getting really cranky.

"Why don't you take Merry and Tyler home while I give Nick a lift?" Keira suggested to her brother.

"If you're sure you don't mind." Douglas was clearly relieved. "I didn't think about getting home when I offered to bring him tonight. I suppose I could make two trips like I did earlier but it is late and…"

"There's no need to go to all that trouble and cut short your time with Merry. I can drive Nick. If that's all right with him."

"Absolutely." Nick sent a wry grin toward the fussy boy.

"You should see him when he's *really* overtired." Merry picked up the child's jacket and started to thread his arms into the sleeves.

Aiden interrupted, his voice gruff and louder than normal. "Ryan's going out, anyway. He can drive Nick home."

"No way, Dad," Keira shot back. "This poor man has already sat through hours of reminiscences about people he doesn't know and all your political rhetoric besides. He deserves a chance to unwind and I know he won't get a break if he rides with Ryan."

She could tell that their war of wills was amusing Nick. Normally, she deferred to Aiden as the family patriarch but she wasn't afraid to challenge him if necessary. Like now.

As she glanced around at her siblings, she noted that they seemed to be waiting to see who would blink first, her or their father.

It was Aiden. He blew out a noisy sigh. "Have it your way. You will, anyway. Just see that you come right back or I'll put out an APB on you."

She leaned to kiss the older man on his cheek, then led the way to the hall where she handed Nick his jacket before getting one for herself. "Ready?"

"Oh, yeah."

"You were ready hours ago, weren't you? I guess the Fitzgeralds can be kind of intimidating when too many of us are in one place."

She donned her own wrap and headed for her police SUV. "Try to remember that this is our idea of what's right and normal, even if it does seem odd to you. Our family sticks together. We may have our differences from time to time, like any group does, but we love each other a lot."

"I could see that," Nick said.

"Was it really so bad?"

"Well…" he drawled, "except for the time you took me

into the kitchen to meet the housekeeper and those few minutes when I was in the yard looking for the vandal who threw that rock, I felt kind of like a bug stuck under a magnifying glass."

"Oh, dear. I am sorry."

"It's okay. They are an interesting bunch."

"And you haven't met them all yet," she replied as she drove down Main toward the shore. "But you will. I expect just about everyone to show up for the Valentine's Day Chocolate Extravaganza. It's the first one Victoria has ever held at the inn."

"Hey, if the food is half as good as what Irene fixed tonight I'll be happy as a clam. I've never had a better meal of Yankee pot roast."

"I'll be sure to tell her. She really tries to please."

"I got the impression she'd do just about anything for your dad."

"For all of us," Keira said, casting a sidelong glance his way. "You're starting to sound like Aunt Vanessa. Believe me, Dad only had eyes for my mother."

"But she's gone now. Maybe you wouldn't have to worry about him being lonely if he gave Irene a chance."

"No way. He and my mother had something special that only comes along once in a lifetime. When she got so sick, he was devastated."

"I'm sorry," Nick said, and Keira could tell he truly meant it.

Her vision misted for a moment as she replied, "We all are."

"Do you want to come in?" Nick asked when she stopped in front of the condo.

"Why?"

It was the half scared, half incredulous look on Keira's face that made him laugh aloud and raise one hand as if taking a vow. "I wasn't getting out of line, I promise. I just wondered if you wanted to help me go over the digital file I downloaded from the funeral. We haven't had time to do it before and I hate to bring my laptop to the office and work there."

"Why?" she asked again, this time with humor twinkling in her eyes. "Don't you like sharing desk space with me?"

"Truthfully, I'd rather sit out in the car than try to keep that little cubbyhole of yours straightened up. I don't know how you do it."

"Poorly," Keira said. She shut off the engine. "Okay. Dad won't call out the troops if I don't stay too long."

As Nick led the way toward the condo, he started to reach to cup her elbow, then stopped himself. This was strictly a business meeting, nothing more, and the farther he stayed from Keira, the better. Her brother would be coming home soon, which was definitely for the best. The last thing he wanted to do was inadvertently sully her reputation. If he knew anything about life in a small town, it was that gossip traveled at supersonic speed.

"Want to leave the door open till Douglas gets here?" Nick asked.

"That won't be necessary. It's cold out and we're planning to behave ourselves." She hesitated barely a heartbeat. "We are, aren't we?"

"Scout's honor," Nick said, holding up his hand as if taking another oath. "I just want to be certain I can ID everybody I photographed at the cemetery. I think I know most of the principal characters but there are a few I can't place."

"Gotcha. I'm ready." She was stripping off her jacket and adjusting the hem of the soft, blue sweater over her jeans.

Does she have any idea how pretty she is? Nick wondered. Her brother had been right when he'd suggested that Keira's innocent air would help her in her job. No criminal in his right mind would expect her to be a formidable cop.

As she turned to sling her jacket over the arm of a chair he remarked, "Okay. I give up. Where do you stash your off-duty gun?"

"In an ankle holster," she said, grinning. "Believe me, there is no room for it at my waist."

Nick could feel his face warming tellingly. Next thing he knew, he'd be wishing their friendship could progress to become something more. That was ridiculous, of course. Keira was too nice, too trusting. He wasn't going to do anything beyond the necessities of his work that might shake her confidence in her fellow man. Not if he could possibly help it.

Instead of commenting, he led the way to the small kitchen table where he'd been reviewing the digital photos and pulled out a chair for her. The only way they could both look at the computer screen at the same time was by sitting side by side so he turned the laptop a little to the left and joined her, elbow to elbow.

"We'll begin as the mourners were entering the church. I got a few candid distance shots then. The rest were taken outside, after the service, with the zoom lens."

"Thank you for being so considerate."

"You're welcome." He pointed. "Look at this one in particular. See how upset the younger Hennessy guy was?" Nick enlarged the shot to full screen. "See what I mean?"

"Yes, I do. I suppose that means there's no way we should suspect poor Cooper. He said he and Olivia were dating, so of course he'd be upset."

"I don't know. What if there was a lovers' quarrel that turned physical? It happens. People have been saying the same thing about Charles but he swore he and Olivia were *not* romantically involved and were getting along well."

"And no one thought to question Cooper because we hadn't believed he and Olivia were dating. I see what you're getting at. We'll have to do that."

"Do you think he could have been the object of the love letter Olivia left behind? It was addressed to her 'Sweetheart.'"

"I wonder. None of us even thought of Cooper in that regard. At least I didn't. Dad never mentioned him, either." She huffed. "Burke will hit the ceiling if we bring his son in for questioning. It's sure to make him think we're trying to shift suspicion from our family to his."

"That's only a problem if it's done for the wrong reasons," Nick said flatly.

Keira grew pensive, leaned forward to prop her elbows on the table and cupped her chin in her hands. "I suppose so. Does that mean that if I ask you a personal question for the right reasons you won't take offense?"

"It might. I'd have to hear the question first."

"Yeah. That's what I was afraid of. Let's finish the pictures," Keira said with a noisy sigh. "I'll ask you on my way out. Then, if you decide to slam the door in my face, I'll be in the right place for it."

Nick could only guess what she was alluding to. Several things occurred to him, not the least of which was his record in Boston, and he dearly hoped she wasn't going to come right out and make him lie for the sake of eventual truth. He was basically an honest man and it galled him to have to prevaricate, even for the sake of the common good.

He began to page slowly through the numbered photos, making notes of names Keira provided as they went. Other than the Fitzgeralds, whom he already knew, he learned who belonged to the extended Connolly family and who was part of Mickey Fitzgerald's fire department.

"How about this woman?" Nick asked, pausing the computer to focus on a slim, obviously overwrought blonde seated in the front row next to the flower-draped casket.

"That's Meghan Henry, Olivia's cousin. I told you she was living here now." He heard Keira sigh before she added, "Poor thing."

"Were they close?"

"I don't think so. Not really. I heard they met in Ireland when they were girls and Olivia contacted Meghan when she came to the U.S."

"Did anyone question her?"

"Not officially. She wasn't around when Olivia died."

"Doesn't matter. She may know something that will help. I'll want to interview her ASAP."

"Okay. I can get in touch with her and set up an appointment if you want."

They both froze when they heard a car door slam. "Sounds like your brother is home."

"Yes. I wonder how long it will take him to check to see why I'm still..."

A loud, abrupt rapping on the door interrupted her.

"About a second and a half," Nick said, then called out, "Come on in. It's open."

Judging by the stern expression on the captain's face, he'd expected something more intimate than the scene that greeted him. His face turned lobster-crimson. "Sorry to bother you. I just wondered if something was wrong when I saw Keira's car."

"You thought you'd need to defend my honor," she teased. "Thanks for looking out for me. I'm fine. We're just working. Nick took some photos at the memorial service and I'm helping him put names with the faces."

"Okay. My mistake." He arched his brows and stared pointedly at his sister. "You planning to stay long? Because if you are, you'd better tell Dad before he actually does call out the troops."

"I think we're almost done," Keira said. "Why don't you phone him for me so you can assure him Nick is behaving himself?"

"Chicken?"

"Sure am," she replied easily. "I'd rather you listened to his lecture than I did. Tell him I'll start home in half an hour or so. I promise."

Giving them both a casual salute, Douglas backed out and shut the door.

"I know you aren't afraid of your father. I saw the way you stood up to him back at the house."

"You're right. I'm not. But Dad tends to run his family a lot like he runs the police department. He'll be halfway through a lecture before he realizes he's talking to one of his kids instead of an out-of-line underling. He doesn't mean to be so hard on us. It's just his way."

"Must have been difficult for your mother," Nick suggested.

"Not really. She accepted his ways because she knew he loved her dearly."

The same way other members of your family accept each other, failings, quirks and all, Nick mused. That kind of unqualified approval was foreign to him. The only time in recent memory he'd heard it put into words was in Pastor Larch's sermon during the memorial service. Nick remembered every detail, particularly the part about the accessibility of God's love and forgiveness to anyone who sought it.

At that time Nick had wondered how such a concept could be put into practice. Now that he'd spent an evening among the Fitzgeralds, however, he was beginning to develop a glimmer of understanding.

These folks didn't seem to judge each other the way his

parents had judged him. It wasn't merely a matter of getting good grades in school and staying out of trouble. It was much more, as if every breath Nick took had to be closely examined and critiqued.

To be fair, he knew he'd often been harder on himself than any outside influence had been, yet he also realized that he had never felt the kind of belonging he'd sensed that evening.

If he hadn't been sent to Fitzgerald Bay to investigate the police department, if he'd simply transferred, he wondered if he'd have eventually found a way to fit in the way his partner did.

Imagining such a thing made him yearn for a chance to go back and change the past. To come to Fitzgerald Bay as the helpful officer he was pretending to be and never have to worry about someone revealing his true nature, his actual job.

Realizing the ridiculousness of such thoughts, Nick shook them off. He was what he was. And he was good at it. That was enough. It would have to be.

The touch of Keira's hand on his forearm startled him out of his reverie.

There was kindness and concern in her expression when she asked, "Are you okay?"

"Yeah. Fine. Just tired, I guess." He clicked rapidly through the final few shots. "That's the lot of them. Thanks for your help."

"You're welcome." She pushed back from the table and got to her feet. "I should be going, anyway. Want me to pick you up in the morning or will you ride in with Douglas again?"

"Might as well go with him." Nick escorted her toward the door. "What was the personal question you were going to ask me after we finished the photos?"

"What? Oh, I forget. It couldn't have been important."

Snagging her jacket as she passed the chair where she'd laid it, she quickly slipped it on while Nick assisted.

"You don't have to be afraid to talk to me," he said softly, hoping there was enough tenderness in his voice to calm her, to encourage her to trust him.

"I'm not afraid," Keira insisted. "If I can take on my father, nobody else will ever scare me."

"Okay. Have it your way." He reached past her to open the door and in doing so felt the warmth of her breath tickle his cheek.

A shiver ran through him from head to toe. His pulse sped. Notions of what it might be like to lean a few inches closer and brush his lips across hers flashed into his mind as if he were suddenly opening his eyes to behold a brilliant summer sunrise.

Nick straightened, relying on well-practiced formality to rescue him. "Shall I walk you to your car?"

"That won't be necessary," Keira said, making no move toward the street.

"You're sure?"

Why didn't she go? Did she know how hard it was for him to keep from hugging her, from kissing her? The innocence in her expression told him she didn't have a clue.

Finally, after long seconds, she took one step. "Well, good night, then. See you Monday morning."

Nick watched, unable and unwilling to take his eyes off her as she made her way to her car and climbed in. He didn't close the apartment door until she was well on her way.

Then he shut it quietly and leaned his back against it, thinking, wondering, lost in the emotions he kept denying. This was bad. Real bad. And it promised to get a lot worse unless he controlled himself better.

So far, Keira had no idea he was beginning to care for her, and that was the way it was going to stay. Period. He didn't dare step over the line and act on his feelings or they'd both be sorry.

Worse, it would come to hurt her terribly. Once she found out he was an undercover agent, she was bound to think any romantic overtures had been made to gain her confidence rather than because the attraction between them was genuine.

Nick closed his eyes, pictured her innocent expression and felt a pang of regret hit him like a punch in the stomach. He did care. He was already too far gone to help himself but that didn't mean he couldn't shelter Keira.

It would mean more than simply watching her back in the field and making sure she stayed safe and well.

It would mean defending her heart from an even worse pain, the kind that grew from disappointment in a loved one and sometimes lasted a lifetime.

It would mean protecting her from himself.

THIRTEEN

Keira had spotted Meghan Henry at church Sunday morning and had asked if she might interview her at home the following day. Although Meghan had not seemed eager, she had nevertheless agreed.

"I'm glad the weather is halfway decent," Keira told Nick that Monday morning as they approached. "Meghan's cottage is down by the beach and the wind off the ocean can be nasty, especially in the winter."

"At least spring isn't far off." His eyebrows arched. "Wow. She found a really nice house. It's New England style, right?"

"Yes." Parking, Keira joined him for the walk up the gracefully curving path to the front door. "It's the kind of place I'd like to own someday. Not too big, not too small, with a homey character and lots of room for flowerbeds."

"I can see you living in a house like this. It suits you."

"Thanks." Keira knocked.

A slim blonde woman answered the door.

"Hello, again," Keira said with a hint of a smile to help put the other woman at ease. "Thank you for seeing us. As you know, I'm Officer Fitzgerald. This is Lieutenant Delfino."

"All right. Come in."

As Meghan stepped back, Keira sensed that she wasn't happy to have company. Word around town was that the newcomer was even less outgoing than her late cousin, Olivia, had been, although there was a definite family resemblance.

"Can I offer you tea? Coffee?" Meghan asked.

"Thank you, no." Nick removed his hat, seated himself on the sofa and opened his small notebook. "This will only take a few minutes. We understand you work from home. Is that correct?"

"Yes. I'm a freelance journalist among other things."

She perched on the edge of a side chair as Keira made herself comfortable at the end of the sofa opposite Nick. They had already agreed that he would take the lead in the interview, then open it to his partner when he thought the time was right. It was hard for Keira to sit still and be patient when so many unanswered questions kept popping into her head.

Pen poised, Nick asked, "What brings you to Fitzgerald Bay, Ms. Henry?"

The other woman's eyes widened. "You must be joking."

"Let me rephrase that," Nick said calmly. "Of course we're sorry for your loss. What I meant was, why did you decide to relocate at this particular time? After all, your cousin is gone."

"But not forgotten," Meghan said as her hands clasped tightly in her lap. "Never forgotten. Her mother is dead. I may be the only close relative Olivia has left who cares that she was murdered. I intend to stay right here and make sure her killer is brought to justice."

"I understand some benevolent townspeople helped you pay for the memorial service and interment. How did that come about, if I may ask?"

It took all the self-control Keira possessed to keep from jumping into the conversation at that point. Nick knew perfectly well who had paid for everything. So why was he asking again?

"Pastor Larch arranged it when I explained that I'd have to

secure a personal loan in order to bury poor Olivia. I never asked where the funds came from. Should I have?"

"Not necessarily."

Nick continued to ask questions for which they already had answers, calming Keira's fears. She supposed it was common practice to try to trip up the only known relative of the deceased; it just seemed a bit silly.

"So, you and Olivia met as children," Nick continued.

"Yes. Several times. In Ireland." The young woman kept her fingers twined tightly together and seemed to be struggling to hold still as Nick continued to question her. Moreover, the more Nick talked, the edgier Meghan acted.

Finally she stood and said, "I really must be getting back to work. Thank you for stopping by instead of making me come to the station. I hope you find clues to Olivia's murder and catch her killer. We all need to know what really happened."

"That, we do," Nick said, leading the way to the door with Keira. He turned and offered his hand to Meghan. "We'll keep in touch, ma'am. I don't have any business cards but if you think of anything else, anything at all, please contact the police department directly. They'll put me in touch with you."

"You're not related to the Fitzgeralds, are you?" she asked, staring past him at Keira and pointedly refusing to shake his hand.

"No. I'm on loan from Boston. Why?"

"Because I'd like to see justice done," Meghan said, "and I wonder if that's even possible in this town."

"I promise you I'll personally do all I can to find answers," Nick vowed.

Meghan finally took his hand, shaking it briefly, as she said, "Then I wish you the best."

They were in the patrol vehicle and headed down the road

before Keira expressed the opinion she'd been holding back. "She seemed awfully nervous. I think she might know more than she's admitting. Either that or she's scared because of what happened to her cousin."

"You're absolutely right," Nick said.

"You really think so?" Keira couldn't have been more pleased if he'd recommended her for instant promotion.

"Yes, I do. Don't look so shocked. I can tell you have the kind of basic instinct that makes a good cop."

"You can?"

Chuckling, he shook his head. "Yes, I can. And I can also tell you're getting much better at controlling your emotional reactions, although I did wonder if you were going to jump up off that couch and start lecturing me a time or two."

"I had complete control of myself," she insisted. "Well, almost."

"You're doing fine for a rookie."

"Thanks. Coming from you that means a lot more than it does when my brothers say it. They *have* to like me."

Nick's laughter filled the car and lifted Keira's spirits higher than ever. In her deepest heart all she'd ever really wanted to be was a cop—a good cop—and hearing praise from a veteran like Nick was akin to seeing the sun break through a bank of gloomy clouds over the Atlantic, bathing the shore in beams of light that made the sand glimmer like gold and tipped the waves with silver.

She didn't need the arrival of spring to make her feel euphoric. Not when she had a partner like this.

In spite of careful analysis, there were no telltale clues on the rock that had shattered the window and interrupted Aiden's family gathering.

That didn't surprise Nick. Rough surfaces seldom retained prints and, given the seeming triviality of the crime, there was no call for further laboratory examination. Besides, since there had been so many people in the house at the time of the incident, the condemnation "Liar" could have been meant for almost anyone.

Nick and Keira were sharing her crowded desk in a back corner of the main police station while he made a list of the oddities they had encountered.

"Okay. I've checked all the official reports but I want you to think back to a month or so before the break-in at the inn," he said quietly, his pen poised over scratch paper. "Did anything else happen around that time that struck you as strange?"

"Other than Olivia's murder, you mean? Nothing. I already told you about Douglas's problems regarding Merry and Tyler, her little boy. You met them at Dad's. Now that Tyler's father is incarcerated and his mother is deceased, there shouldn't be any more trouble in that regard."

"Okay. The next thing was my arrival and my room being ransacked. Is that right?"

"Right. Then you and I were followed. I would have ended up as roadkill if you hadn't pulled me out of the way."

Nick was twirling his pen, mulling over the list. She leaned closer and tilted her head to peer at the paper. "What's next?"

"The biggie. The man-made avalanche."

Noting the way Keira shifted her position to draw slightly away from him, Nick focused an intent look on her face, then reached to lay one hand over hers. "What is it? You just thought of something else, didn't you? I can see it in your eyes."

"You must be imagining things."

"No. I'm not. Talk to me, Keira. What is it? Did you remember something about Charles? Is that why you won't confide in me?"

She jerked away. "Of course not! How dare you say such a terrible thing?"

"Then enlighten me. Prove me wrong." Nick leaned back and laced his fingers behind his head in a purposely nonchalant pose. "I'm listening."

"You have no idea. You just have no idea." Her chair went skidding when she stood abruptly. "Excuse me. I'll be back in a minute."

Watching her walk stiffly away, Nick was struck by a sense of loss and sadness that surprised him. It was obvious his partner was hiding something. But what? If they assumed that all the unusual incidents were connected, there was no way they could lay the blame on Charles. After all, he'd been in the house with the others when the rock had sailed through the window.

What about everything else? Nick shook his head. He'd decided long ago that there was no way any of the Fitzgeralds would take the chance of endangering Keira by pushing a boulder off a cliff while she was below. An out-of-town detective might be fair game but they'd never harm one of their own.

That conclusion wasn't enough to prove to anyone that the FBPD was totally on the up-and-up but it went a long way toward convincing Nick. Because his partner had been involved in the attempt on their lives at the murder scene, he was positive none of her extended family could have been responsible.

If only the others had been successful in lifting discernible prints from the snowplow. Unfortunately, Aiden himself had insisted that there was nothing usable. That left them all in the dark.

Across the room, Keira was disappearing into the chief's office. She closed the door behind her.

Puzzled, Nick just sat there and stared. What had she remembered? And why was she in such a hurry to share it with her father? That reaction did not bode well for the department's claim of impartiality and straightforward investigation. Not well at all.

"I need to tell him," Keira insisted. "He's about to figure it out, anyway, and if we keep him in the dark any longer he might get hurt."

"Not yet," Aiden insisted. "I want to have time to probe deeper into his record first. His file is too clean. Too perfect. I have the sense there's something rotten going on."

"Not with Nick. He's wonderful."

The look her father shot her way was anything but approving. "We'll see about that. Has he been any help in the murder investigation?"

"How would I know? I'm just a dumb rookie, remember?"

"You're not dumb, Keira, but you are too gullible. I don't want you to get hurt."

"You know I'm always careful, more so now that I've been partnered with Nick. Besides, he's saved my neck at least once."

"I didn't mean what's happened in the line of duty," the chief said solemnly, his voice husky. "I meant in your personal life. I think you may like Delfino too much for your own good."

"I'll take that warning under advisement," she said, managing a smile only because she knew her father had her best interests at heart. "I'm a big girl, Dad." The smile widened. "And I'm armed. I can take care of myself."

"I hope so," Aiden replied. "Even the best of us can sometimes be led astray."

"I'm not going to let Nick lead me anywhere. Well, except to the Valentine's Day Chocolate Extravaganza on the fourteenth. Are you going?"

"Yes, primarily because it will be good for me politically. You know your mother was the party person in the family."

"Burke and his cronies will be there so you have to show up, too. Gotcha."

Keira sighed as she reached for the doorknob and prepared to return to her desk. "Are you sure I can't tell Nick we got a hit on those snowplow prints? He probably has a perfectly logical explanation why someone else from Boston is in town. For all we know the perp may be Nick's enemy."

"Or his buddy." Aiden was shaking his head slowly, decisively. "As soon as I hear back from a few friends on the force, I'll let you know. In the meantime, see that you follow my orders."

Saluting with a snap and a grin, Keira agreed. When she turned away, however, her smile vanished. Partners didn't keep things from each other. Not when they shared the kind of trust she and Nick had developed already.

Well, it couldn't be helped. She'd tell him about the fingerprints and apologize profusely just as soon as she got permission. And until then she was going to do all in her power to steer Nick away from trouble. It was the least she could do.

To her relief, when she returned to her desk, her partner was nowhere in sight. In his place was a terse note that simply said, "See you after lunch," with no details and no invitation to join him. Oh, well. Even if he was mad at her, she figured he'd keep his promise to attend the Valentine's party.

She already had the perfect outfit for it, too. A silky, filmy, knee-length red dress that was totally out of character and guaranteed to knock Nick's socks off. Hopefully, he'd still be in awe when she finally got permission to tell him whose prints were found on the plow that had pushed that boulder down on top of them.

The way Keira saw it, the more her partner admired her

as an individual, the less likely he was to stay angry when he learned he'd been lied to by the cop side of her personality.

Satisfied with that logic she grabbed her jacket, made sure she had enough cash with her to purchase the tickets and walked across Main Street.

Since it was noon and the Sugar Plum Café was packed, as usual, she decided to stop at the desk of the inn.

Victoria Evans looked as if she relished all the hustle and bustle. Her golden-brown curls were bouncing and her brown eyes bright.

"Hi, Keira! What's up?"

"I came to buy tickets for your chocolate party on the four-teenth."

"Tickets? Plural? Well, well."

"Now you're starting to sound like my family. I invited my new partner so he could meet more people." Keira couldn't help grinning. "That's all there is to it."

"Right." The Sugar Plum's owner reached into a drawer behind the counter and brought out two crimson pieces of cardboard. "My daughter helped me make these so I hope you don't mind the glitter flaking off. Paige insisted we add it."

"Not a problem." Tucking them into her shirt pocket, Keira handed over the correct change then dusted stray silver bits off her fingers. "I imagine most of my family will attend." She paused for emphasis before pointedly adding, "Even Owen."

"That's nice."

"That's all you have to say?"

Coloring slightly, Victoria didn't comment. There had been a time, over ten years ago, when Keira had hoped Owen would make Victoria Evans a part of their family. That had been before Victoria's alcoholic father had killed a Fitzger-ald cousin while driving drunk. The loss of then seventeen-year-old Patrick Fitzgerald, one of Mickey's sons, had hit the whole family hard.

Soon after that, Victoria had left town and no one had heard from her until recently when she'd returned with her nine-year-old daughter, Paige. As far as Keira was concerned, the poor woman was nearly as much a victim of her drunken father's sins as her cousin Patrick had been.

"Okay," Keira said with a sigh, "have it your way. What are you planning to wear? I have a knockout red dress."

"I'll be spending most of my time in the kitchen, anyway so it really won't matter."

"Well, I'm certainly looking forward to tasting more of your delicious pastries."

"That's my plan," Victoria said with a smile. "Devious, huh?"

"Very. Well, see you."

As she was turning to leave Victoria said, "He's in the dining room."

"Who is?"

"Your yummy partner, as if you didn't know."

"Actually, I didn't. He said he'd see me after lunch but he didn't mention where he was planning to eat."

The proprietor snickered. "Some detective you are. The guy's on foot. Where else would he go?"

"It's only a couple blocks to the marina. He could have walked down there."

"Only he didn't. Are you going to join him?"

The idea was tempting but Keira wanted more time to herself while she struggled to justify keeping possibly important information from Nick.

She shook her head. "Not today. Besides, I need to watch my waistline if I intend to fit into my red dress."

"Then I suppose you aren't interested in sampling one of

the new recipes I'm planning on using for the party. It's a chocolate tart with raspberry topping."

"For you, I'll make the sacrifice," Keira joked. "But wrap it up for me, will you? I need to run a few errands before I stop to eat."

"Okay. Follow me." Victoria led the way past the busy café hostess and into the kitchen.

Keira's attention was momentarily diverted by an intense urge to catch a glimpse of Nick. As she passed the doorway to the dining area, she could see some of the tables but he wasn't seated at any of those. Judging by the reflections in the glass covering the myriad framed photos hanging on the walls in that room, every table was full. It was simply impossible to make out Nick's face amid that overlapping jumble of images.

"He's sitting back in the corner by the potted palm," Victoria teased. "Of course, you're not a bit interested. Right?"

"Right."

Keira didn't care that she was blushing. Not when there was no one to see her rosy cheeks but Victoria. She had always shared a sisterly affection for the other woman, even when so many others were condemning her unjustly because of her father. No one could choose their relatives. Perhaps given a more stable home life, Victoria wouldn't have felt compelled to flee Fitzgerald Bay in the first place.

The kitchen was busy yet pristine, just the way Keira remembered it. "Mmm. Everything smells wonderful."

"Thanks. We try. Here are the tarts. Is one enough?"

"Plenty, thanks." Accepting a white bag containing the chocolaty treat, she offered payment.

"Nonsense. It's on the house. I just want your honest opinion and I know you'll tell me the truth."

"Of course," Keira replied, embarrassed to be lauded for her honesty when her biggest current problem was how to follow orders and withhold the truth from her partner without going against her own sense of right and wrong.

It wasn't going to be easy.

Then again, what worthwhile task in life was?

FOURTEEN

Nick finally managed to reach his covert Boston contact while he was dressing for the Valentine's party.

"Evening, Chief. Glad I finally got through. It's Nick Delfino."

"About time you called in. I was sure I'd hear from you after we sent the results of the prints you lifted."

"What prints?"

"Whoa," the chief drawled. "Let's start over. Did you or did you not almost get crowned with a rock the size of a city bus?"

"It was more smart-car size but yeah. Somebody stole a snowplow and shoved a boulder over a cliff while I was examining the shore below."

"Right. And they lifted prints off the plow."

"I'd heard there was nothing usable."

"Oh? Who told you that, the department you're supposed to be investigating?"

"As a matter of fact, yes."

"Well, you'd better sit down, Delfino. Those prints belonged to your favorite fugitive, Anthony Carlton."

"What?" Staggered, Nick sank onto the edge of his bed and stared, unseeing, while he tried to reason.

"I said…"

"I heard you. Who did you tell?"

"Talked to the Fitzgerald Bay chief myself. At least, that's who he said he was. I had no reason to doubt him."

"And you told him you had a positive ID?"

"Yes. He asked for more info on Carlton so I'm going to send it—as soon as I clean it up so your name isn't in the file."

"Thanks. That's comforting."

"I'd ask how the investigation is coming if I didn't sense the answer already. Do you think they made you? Is that why they're withholding information?"

"I don't think so." His frown deepened. "I can't see any good reason why they'd lie to me about that." *Or why my supposedly supportive partner would be a party to it,* he added. Was that what had been bugging Keira? Was that the dilemma she'd been struggling with?

"Well, good luck figuring it out. Just watch your back, Nick. If Carlton is still around there, and I have no reason to think he isn't, you're in danger."

"So is my partner and the whole department," he said flatly. "That's why the secrecy makes no sense. Can you email me the file you alter so I don't make any mistakes when I bring it up for discussion?"

"Sure. On its way. The only reason we gave the ID info to the FBPD in the first place is because the original lab request came from them. Keep in closer touch, okay? I don't want any more slipups."

"Hey, if you'd stop taking time off I'd be able to reach you in a timely manner."

"What's that supposed to mean? I haven't had a vacation in years. You know I'm lucky to get a free weekend."

Nick gritted his teeth. Things were starting to make more sense. "Then you'd better monitor incoming calls more closely," Nick said. "I've been trying to reach you for over

a week. Something tells me my messages are being inter-
cepted."

"I'll take care of it. We'll get this office cleaned up if it's
the last thing we do."

As Nick bid him goodbye and powered up his laptop, he
found himself hoping that innocent vow didn't turn out to be
prophetic.

Pirouetting in front of the mirror in the Sugar Plum's
powder room, Keira was already so nervous she had the hiccups. Her dress was perfect, her hair was perfect, her makeup
was perfect and she'd even let Fiona do her nails although
she'd insisted they be kept short so she could draw and fire
her gun without hindrance.

Nick had agreed to meet at the party, meaning Keira was
going to be able to let him see her for the first time without
a heavy coat or her snow boots.

Picturing herself in clunky winter-weather boots below the
handkerchief hem of the filmy red dress made her chuckle.
There was definitely an advantage to wearing the right shoes.
If Nick hadn't been a good five inches taller than she was, she
might have opted for a lower heel. Thankfully, she'd been able
to choose a perfect height to set off her shapely legs without
feeling unbalanced.

Now, if she could only stop wanting to giggle all the time,
she'd be in good shape. Every time she envisioned the upcoming festivities, her grin spread so wide her cheeks hurt.

"By the time of the party, I'm going to be exhausted from
all this smiling," she told herself, immediately laughing again
at such a silly thought.

Tonight was the night. Tonight she'd warn Nick in spite
of the chief's orders to the contrary. There had to be a way.
There had to be. Even if she wasn't certain how to accom-

plish it, she was going to tell him about the fingerprint ID. Somehow.

Taking a deep breath and closing her eyes, Keira laid a hand on the edge of the sink for balance and began to pray. "Father, I really need help. I don't know what's right and what's wrong. I should, but I don't."

Another breath. Another sigh. "But *You* know. And You know how badly I want to be honest with everyone. The trouble is, I'm stuck between two truths, two loyalties. Help me? Guide me? Please?"

The only answer she received was in the form of a couple of twittering, texting teenage girls who burst through the door and interrupted her peace and quiet.

Perhaps that was enough of an answer, Keira thought. It was time to venture out into the elaborately decorated dining room where the others were gathering and wait there for Nick.

If she hadn't been so nervous that she was afraid to eat, she'd have looked forward to all that chocolate. As it was, however, the strong, sweet odor was almost overwhelming. She knew she'd have more hiccups—or worse—if she dared down a single bite.

Later, after she and Nick had had a chance to talk privately and she'd made him understand her dilemma, maybe they could share a table and enjoy the pastries. Until then, however, she figured she'd better just hang out with the crowd and try to look relaxed. If she could manage to appear even a smidgen more poised than she felt, she'd be thrilled.

"And totally amazed," Keira muttered as she left the ladies' room.

Victoria was greeting guests at the door while Charlotte Newbright, her hostess, checked paid admissions.

"These are for me and a guest," Keira told Charlotte as she handed her the glittery tickets.

"Say no more." The chubby woman patted at her spiked hairdo and winked. "I know exactly who to watch for."

Keira was positive her cheeks had turned as crimson as her dress. Victoria knew. Charlotte knew. Chances were that most of the people who would be in attendance tonight also knew. Well, too bad. Keira wasn't ashamed of being attracted to Nick and hopefully he wouldn't be sorry to hear their names joined during conversations. That kind of thing was bound to happen in a group this familiar with each other.

He was going to have to learn to accept small-town ways if and when they ever became a true couple. That was another element of his personality that worried her. The man was a born outsider, even in his own family. Could he ever come to terms with having his private life so public?

"I'll worry about that later," Keira whispered to herself.

Standing tall and pausing to scan the room, she spotted her sister, Fiona, beneath a bunch of red-and-white balloons that sported matching paper streamers. It was good to see her laughing and talking to some of the handsome firemen who had once worked with her late husband. Jimmy Cobb's friends continued to look after Fiona as if they were part of her extended family, which, in a way, they were.

Waving at Fiona she began to thread her way toward her across the crowded room, greeting others as she passed. Hanging out with her sister was probably a clear sign of apprehension but right now Keira desperately craved moral support.

They had just met and exchanged hugs when Fiona pointed past her. "Look over there. See who just came in?"

Keira's breath went out of her. She wobbled slightly on her unfamiliar high heels.

Her gaze met Nick's and locked on.

She saw his eyes widen and his jaw drop for a second before he recovered and started toward her.

It was all she could do to stand still and wait for him.

Until Fiona whispered, "Steady, girl," in her ear Keira forgot to smile. That silly prompt broke the ice and made her grin.

Nick was almost there before Keira realized he was not returning her expression of friendship. Nevertheless, he looked better than ever. He'd donned a sport jacket and seemed more like an ordinary man than he did a fellow officer—if you could consider anything about Nick Delfino ordinary.

Keira couldn't. As far as she was concerned, she only had eyes for one guy in the entire room and he was coming to a stop right in front of her.

If Nick hadn't started out so upset, he might have had more trouble keeping Keira at arm's length. The woman had undergone a transformation he would never have dreamed possible. Where before he'd thought of her as very pretty and sweet, she was now the most exotically beautiful creature he had ever laid eyes on.

And she looked so happy, he hated to spoil her mood. Perhaps his planned confrontation could wait a little while longer. After all, the evening was just getting started.

Allowing his instincts free rein he shook her hand. "Excuse me, ma'am. Have you seen my partner, Officer Fitzgerald? She's supposed to meet me here."

"Is she? Can you describe her?"

Nick could not help grinning. He just hoped he didn't look as befuddled as he felt. His gaze traveled rapidly from her head to her toes and he tried to make his assessment humorous in spite of the fact he would gladly have stood there for hours taking in the amazing sight of her transformation.

"Well," Nick drawled, "to start with she's shorter than you are." He openly admired her. "Where in the world did you stash your sidearm?"

"I'm afraid I couldn't find a place to wear it tonight and it wouldn't fit in my fancy clutch bag." She nervously brushed her hands over her hips, smoothing a skirt that hung so gracefully it needed no adjustment.

"Can't say I'm surprised. That dress doesn't look like it has a lot of spare room for a holster."

"Nope. It was guaranteed to knock your socks off, though. Are your toes getting cold yet?"

"Undoubtedly." Noticing that their conversation was garnering far more attention than he liked, he took her hand and drew her aside with, "Let's get something to eat and drink, shall we?"

Keira's free hand settled at her waist. "I don't think my stomach can handle food right now but a cup of punch would be nice. I guess I'm a little nervous."

"I can understand that." Nick handed her a small red plastic cup filled with cherry-colored liquid. "If I had your guilty conscience I wouldn't be able to eat much, either."

"My *what?*"

He had to briefly steady her hand to keep her from sloshing her drink. "You heard me. Like I said, let's find a nice quiet corner where we can talk, shall we?"

"Okay."

"And *smile,* Keira," he added, urging her along with his hand at her elbow. "You look as if I'm leading you to the gallows."

"I do want to talk to you, Nick, but there's a problem."

"I'll make it easy for you. I already know you've been lying to me."

He felt her steps falter and tightened his hold to offer more support.

Instead of accepting his help the way he'd expected her to, Keira jerked her arm away and nearly spilled the cup of punch.

"It's not like that," she insisted. "You have no idea what I've been going through."

"Then maybe you'd better tell me."

Finding a small table in the farthest corner of the crowded room, Nick held a chair for Keira, then scooted his seat closer to hers so he could watch the crowd while they talked. Nobody was going to sneak near enough to eavesdrop. Not if he had anything to say about it.

Beside him, his partner sat trembling. She was upset, all right, but that couldn't be helped. Once she broke down and explained exactly what was going on, he'd decide what his next move would be.

He leaned closer, noticing the scent of roses that was wafting from Keira's silky hair and the way her eyes seemed so innocent, so astonishingly beautiful. They were bluer than a summer sky and fringed with lashes that he imagined brushing against his cheek with feathery softness.

It took special effort to steel himself and say, "All right. We're alone. Talk."

"I will." Her sigh was audible and seemed terribly sad. "You said you already knew, so why aren't you lecturing me?"

"Because I want to hear the whole story from you. Why did you keep the truth from me? You and your brothers know who tried to kill us on the beach. Am I right?"

Keira nodded. "Yes. We were under strict orders to not tell you yet."

She set aside her drink and grasped his hand so tightly he could feel her nails pressing into his palm.

"Orders? From whom?" Nick asked.

"The chief. When Dad got the results back from IAFIS and learned that the perp was from Boston, he started wondering if you were connected. He's trying to find out more before he confronts you but he insisted you be kept in the dark until then."

"Who did he say the prints belonged to?"

"A fugitive named Anthony Carlton. But you know that, don't you?"

"Yes."

"What's his connection to you?"

"Nothing that will affect my work here, especially now that I know who and what we're dealing with in addition to the Henry murder."

Hesitating, he laid his other hand over where their fingers were already entwined. "I will ask for a different partner, or maybe none at all. I know my way around town well enough by now to handle further interviews alone."

Keira looked stricken. "Oh, please don't do that. I didn't want to keep anything from you. Honest I didn't. I know you're mad at me right now but I was going to tell you tonight. I just hadn't figured out how to keep my promise to my father and still warn you to be on guard."

Nick began to shake his head as he patted her hand. "It's not that, Keira. I'm not banishing you. I'm trying to protect you. Carlton can be ruthless. If it's true he's come to Fitzgerald Bay and is still here, I don't want you caught in the line of fire."

"Then it's not a coincidence," she said, staring into his eyes. "He is out to get you."

"Let's just say I'm not his favorite person and leave it at that."

"No way. How can I—can any of us—help you if we don't know the whole story?"

"I'm not looking for help."

"Tough. You're going to get it, at least from me. Just tell me one thing. Are you clean?"

Sobering, Nick said, "Yes."

"Then that's good enough for me. I'm going to go tell Dad it's time to stop playing games with you. We're going to be straight with each other from now on, or else."

"Is that a threat?" Nick stood when Keira withdrew her hand and abruptly pushed her chair away.

"Think of it as my personal promise," she said, managing to smile even though he could tell there were unshed tears lurking behind those long, lovely lashes.

What now? If he confessed everything, he'd have to leave town voluntarily or be run out by her relatives. If he kept up the ruse for a little while longer, he might be in a better position to speak up.

Considering the fact that he'd been lying to her, to all of them, for weeks, a few more days wouldn't really matter. His goose was cooked either way.

Cupping Keira's elbow he fell into step with her as she headed back into the fray.

All right. Now that he knew Carlton was in the area he'd be doubly cautious. And since Keira and the other officers were also aware of the danger, he could stop worrying that they'd be too careless and get hurt.

But what was he going to do about his partner?

What, indeed? Nick thought, gritting his teeth. It was beginning to look as if he'd have to have a heart-to-heart with Aiden and explain part of the reasons why he didn't want Keira involved.

That was going to be tough to accomplish without going into Carlton's true background but he'd think of something that would suffice. He had to. He wasn't going to set foot on the street again until Keira had been reassigned. Until he knew she was safe from the danger that was shadowing him. He'd miss spending so much time with her but...

Miss it? Nick snorted in disdain. It was going to kill him to be forced to step away from Keira, even for her own good, and he knew it.

FIFTEEN

Keira made a beeline for her father, quickly working her way through the throng by ignoring everyone she passed, Nick right behind her. When she reached Aiden, he was pontificating about the great job he'd do if he were elected mayor to carry on his father Ian's legacy.

"Excuse us, please," Keira said, slipping a hand through her father's elbow and holding tight. "I need to borrow our future mayor for a private chat."

It didn't surprise her at all when the man he'd been addressing seemed greatly relieved.

Aiden cast a warning glance at Nick. "I don't mind talking to you, Keira, but I thought you said you wanted this to be private."

"Nick is included," she said flatly. "Let's step out the back door onto the deck, shall we?"

"You'll freeze."

"She can have my jacket," Nick said, slipping it off and draping it over her shoulders as the three left the dining room. It didn't escape her notice that he'd kept his hands on her shoulders when there was really no need to hold the coat in place.

Aiden stopped abruptly, closed the door on the party and faced them. "All right, Keira. You have my attention." He eyed Nick as if he were a rabid animal about to bare his fangs and go for their throats.

"Nick knows," Keira began before her father interrupted her with a string of unintelligible mutterings.

Nick spoke up to end the chief's tirade. "She didn't tell me a thing. She didn't have to. I happened to talk to a buddy of mine back in Boston this evening and he mentioned getting a hit on the prints the FBPD sent. When were you going to tell *me* about it?"

"As soon as I was sure you weren't mixed up in something shady," Aiden replied. "Now I suppose we'll never know."

"*I* know," Keira insisted.

"Oh? How?" Aiden arched a brow.

"I know Nick is clean because I *asked* him."

Her father laughed wryly. "Good for you. I guess that's as much proof as we can expect until I hear back on my latest query." His gaze was steady and Keira was proud to see that Nick didn't wilt under that kind of pressure the way she often had, especially as a child.

"I take it you've asked for Carlton's rap sheet," Nick said flatly.

"Yes. Is there anything you'd like to tell me before it arrives?"

"Only that the man is dangerous. Now that I know he's around, I think you should reassign Keira."

"My thoughts exactly," the chief said. "I'll put her on desk duty."

"No!" Keira blurted out.

Both men answered in unison with a loud "Yes."

"You'll have use of her patrol vehicle," Aiden added. "Hopefully it won't be for long. Strangers in this town usually stand out like lumps of coal on a snowbank. We'll get him. And when we do, I plan to ask him plenty about you."

"Fine," Nick said. "You do that."

"I will."

Had the conversation taken place between someone like Hank Monroe and Nick, Keira would have expected one of them to have threatened to throw a punch. Since these antagonists were, for the most part, behaving themselves, she decided it was high time to end the confrontation.

"Okay," she said, forcing a smile, "now that that's settled, we can all go back to the party."

Aiden huffed, pivoted without comment, jerked open the door and left them alone on the wooden decking.

Keira felt Nick's arm tighten around her shoulders as she shivered. Instead of following the older man inside, however, he turned her so they were face-to-face.

"Your dad and I are right, you know. It is dangerous."

His gaze was steady and calming, so much so that she closed the distance between them the barest amount and placed her palms flat on his chest as she said, "I know."

"We will catch Carlton. And when we do, I want you to remember that all my actions were for the greater good."

"Of course they are. I know that. I..." She lifted her chin and their lips drew closer, so near that she could feel his warm breath on her face.

Keira froze. Waited. Closed her eyes in anticipation. Nick was going to kiss her. She knew it. She just knew it. She was already in his arms. He was holding her close. All he'd need to do was tilt his head just a tiny bit to one side and...

Suddenly, he thrust her away.

When she managed to focus past the fog of emotion, she could see he was disconcerted. Might he think she was too free with her affection? Certainly not. She had never behaved in any way except professionally around him.

Well, except maybe for the time when she'd saved his life on the shore and had hugged him for a little too long. An experience like that, brought on by cheating death, hardly counted in the overall scheme of things.

As Nick stood and gazed at her, she was overcome with affection and concern. The man almost seemed stricken, as if he were suffering instead of judging her to be lacking in some way.

What would she do, what did she do, whenever her nieces or nephew exhibited similar emotional distress? That was easy. And natural. And so right that Keira refused to question it.

She cupped Nick's warm cheeks, pulled him closer and simply kissed him.

That was when everything changed.

Nick was lost and he knew it. One touch of the lips he'd yearned to taste and he was a goner. Tightening his embrace he leaned over Keira and deepened their kiss.

Although she was returning his show of affection it took her a few moments to truly respond. When she did, it was so amazing it took Nick's breath away. This was a kiss like none other he had ever shared. It was *tender*.

When he finally broke contact and straightened he could tell that he was not the only one who had been stunned. All he could say was, "Wow."

Keira's eyes were misty, her mouth soft and trembling.

"You can say that again."

"Okay. Wow." He began to smile. "I'm sure glad your father wasn't here to see that."

She giggled. "I don't think it would have been quite the same if Dad had been standing there watching us."

"I am sorry," Nick said softly, seriously. "I know it's against the rules to fraternize."

"Then it's a good thing we're not partners anymore," she teased, clearly amused and as euphoric as he was.

"We aren't, are we?"

"Nope."

"But we are still members of the same department."

"Sadly, yes. I suppose now you're going to tell me you don't want to kiss me again."

"I wouldn't go that far," Nick said, setting her away but keeping one arm around her shoulders. "I do think we should go back inside before somebody catches us necking on the porch like a couple of teenagers."

"I never really got around to doing much of that," Keira said, lowering her lashes demurely as they edged toward the door. "I was always too busy with school and chasing around after my big brothers when they played sports. They say I was a real pest."

Nick felt her shoulders shake and couldn't tell if she was laughing or crying so he replied with the kind of comment he figured would solve whatever ailed her.

"That's okay by me," he whispered in her ear. "If you got any better at kissing, you'd have to pick me up off the floor because I'd have fainted dead away."

"It was pretty good, wasn't it?"

He gave her a squeeze. "It was perfect."

The rest of the evening passed in a blur, at least as far as Keira was concerned. The only time she left Nick's side was when she ventured into the ladies' room with Fiona.

"Do I detect a change in the way you and Nick are getting along?" Fiona asked, meeting Keira's gaze in the gilt-framed mirror above the powder-room sink.

"I can't imagine where you got that idea."

"Oh, maybe from the way you've been grinning and looking so goofy whenever he's nearby—which in your case is pretty much all the time."

"He has been sticking close tonight, hasn't he?" She felt

warmth rising to burn her cheeks. "I suppose you wouldn't believe me if I told you he was just protecting me from a bad guy."

"You carry a gun, Keira. How much extra protection do you need?"

"No gun tonight, but I do see your point. I'll take all the TLC Nick wants to hand out, now or later." She covered her mouth with her hand and muted a giggle. "Just don't tell him I admitted it, okay?"

"Okay. Wow. This is the first time I've ever known you to act this way. Are you getting serious about him?"

When Keira didn't answer, Fiona gave a little squeal. "Oh, my! You are, aren't you? I never thought I'd see the day you stopped insisting you didn't need anybody special in your life."

"I guess our relationship could develop into something special. We'll have to wait and see."

"Is that what you want?"

Keira sighed deeply, noisily. "I wish I knew. It's like I'm learning things about myself that I hadn't dreamed were present. It's very unsettling."

"Wanting to be with someone all the time? Wondering what he's doing and if he's thinking of you, too? Wishing he'd hurry back because you miss him like crazy even though you've only been apart for a few minutes?"

"Yes! It's exactly like that."

Fiona was grinning widely and there were unshed tears in her eyes as she hugged her younger sister. "Oh, honey. Brace yourself," she said tenderly. "You're falling in love."

"I'd offer you a ride home if I had my car here," Nick said. He and Keira had paused in the lobby to retrieve their coats and he was helping her on with hers. Her boots sat empty at their feet.

"That's okay. I rode with Dad."

"Bummer. Then you can't give me a ride, either. Douglas and Merry have already left. Tyler pooped out hours ago and they took him home."

"I can always borrow Dad's Lincoln and let him hitch a ride with Granddad. Our house is right on his way home."

"Would you mind?" Nick clasped her hand and felt her fingers intertwining with his. "I'm not ready for this evening to end."

"Neither am I." She gave his hand a quick squeeze. "I think it would be better if I was alone when I asked for the car keys. Wait here. I'll be right back."

Nick watched her walk away and felt his heart clench. This had been an evening he doubted he'd be able to forget even if he tried. Not only had he discovered his true feelings in regard to Keira, he'd been able to casually observe many of the townspeople he'd been planning to interview.

One of the most interesting was Cooper Hennessy. The guy wasn't a lot younger than Nick was but he seemed as lost as a teen when it came to social interaction.

Judging by the tidbits of gossip Nick had managed to glean, Cooper had been in love with Olivia. That certainly explained why he'd acted so distressed at her funeral.

As far as Nick was concerned, the whole Hennessy family was a bit strange, although he supposed it was natural for a successful lawyer and social climber like Burke to choose a younger wife if he intended to start another family, particularly at his age.

Keira returned with a ring of keys in hand. "Got 'em. You ready?"

"Yes," Nick said, although his gaze lingered on the guests remaining in the dining room.

Following his line of sight, Keira possessively took Nick's

arm. "Are you sure you're done ogling bleached blondes? If not, I can wait."

Nick chuckled. "I'm done, believe me. I was just watching Christina Hennessy and thinking about that whole family. Burke's second wife looks like the kind of woman who requires a lot of upkeep, as they say."

"Like a big, fancy house, all the gaudy jewelry she can hang on herself, a new car and a nanny for the baby? Yeah. That about covers it."

"Did she seem distracted to you tonight?" Nick was watching the slim, bejeweled woman staring up at some photographs of townspeople that adorned the walls of the inn. She didn't look happy. Probably was photographed without her diamonds or something.

"More than usual? Not at all. Christina's always been standoffish. She's never fit in here. It's too bad but don't blame it all on us. Some of the church ladies have tried to reach out to her. She's not interested. She even has the nanny bring her toddler to story hour at Fiona's instead of coming herself. If you don't believe me, ask Merry. She works there, too."

Nick picked up Keira's boots and escorted her through the lobby. "I don't need to ask anyone else. I'll take your word for it."

"Thanks. That's a really nice feeling."

"It's not the only nice feeling you've had tonight, I hope." It pleased him to hear her giggle nervously.

"I'm not admitting a thing. Your ego is big enough already."

The cool, salty air and fog enveloped them as they left the inn and paused on the covered porch.

Nick held out the boots. "You'd better put these on unless you want to get snow in the open toes of those red shoes."

"I know. I just hate to spoil the outfit that way."

"Then I'll help," he told her as he swept her into his arms and started down the stairs toward the parking lot. "Just point me in the right direction."

Giggling, Keira wrapped one arm around Nick's neck and hung on to her clutch purse with the other. "The Lincoln. Third on your left."

As soon as he had set her carefully on her feet, Nick opened the door of Aiden's sedan and she slid behind the wheel.

Circling to the passenger side, he wondered if he should try to keep their conversation light, as it had been so far, or broach the subject of their mutual attraction.

Is it too soon for that? Probably. No, undoubtedly, he reasoned, ruing the fact that they had kissed, yet recalling the sweetness of her lips.

He tossed her boots onto the floor in the backseat, then joined her in the front and slammed the door.

Silence reigned.

Keira's small purse lay on the seat between them. Her hands were fisted on the steering wheel and she was staring straight ahead. Was she waiting for him to make the next move?

"I want us to take things slowly," Nick finally ventured. "What happened tonight on the porch shouldn't change the way we treat each other."

"O-o-o-okay," she drawled, casting a lopsided smile his way. "You give that a try and see how it works for you."

Her candor struck him so funny he began to laugh. "You don't think it's possible?"

"Not in a million years. But feel free to treat me as if we've never kissed if that's what you want."

"It is going to be hard to do."

"You betcha it is." Her eyes twinkled in the light from the inn's windows. "It probably is a good thing we're not going to be partners anymore. I didn't like that idea when I first heard it but it will help me keep my mind on my work."

"Do you think your brothers will notice a change?"

"Probably. Fiona already has. It's hard to hide anything from my family, believe me. They have better sonar than Uncle Joe's fish-location gear. They don't miss a thing."

"Keira, I…"

She interrupted. "You don't have to say anything more. I know one little kiss doesn't mean much. I just want you to know I think you're very special, Nick. And I'd like to get to know you better. Even after you finish your work here in Fitzgerald Bay and move on, I'd like to keep in touch. That's okay with you, isn't it?"

"Of course," he said softly, wondering how this amazing, gorgeous woman would feel about him in another week or two.

Humph. She'd probably hate his guts and want to take back her offer of a continuing relationship. He wouldn't blame her for telling him to get lost.

If he were in her place and learned that his trusted partner had been lying from the get-go, that's precisely what he'd do.

To imagine any other outcome regarding this assignment was more than foolish. It was absurd.

SIXTEEN

If Keira had not been familiar with the Fitzgerald Bay streets and known exactly where she was going, the thick fog might have kept her from even attempting the drive.

As it was, she'd slowed the car to a crawl and was leaning against the steering wheel to peer through the windshield. "Pea soup has nothing on this stuff."

"Yeah. I think we're almost there." Nick pointed. "Isn't that the mill's big waterwheel?"

"Right." Inching into the driveway and parking, Keira suddenly frowned. "Wait a minute. What's that shadow?"

"Where?"

"Up there. On the top of the wheel. It almost looks like somebody is messing with the window to your apartment."

"It sure does." He drew his gun from a hidden holster and extended his free arm across the front seat in a blocking motion. "You stay here. Have you got your cell phone with you?"

"In my purse."

"Good. Call the station. And be sure to tell them there's an officer on scene. I don't want to get shot as a prowler."

"I'll back you up."

"No. You won't. You're not armed, remember?" He reached for the door handle. "Turn off the headlights. The minute I get out, he'll be able to see there are two of us because the dome light will flash on. That can't be helped. Keep your head down, make that call, then wait for backup."

Before she could argue, Nick had left the car and dropped into a crouching run. If it hadn't been for the dense fog, she might have been able to see what was happening once he drew closer to the mill. Unfortunately, he'd disappeared into the mist in seconds.

Darkness enveloped her, both literal and emotional. Keira hunched low in the front seat, cupped her cell phone and dialed 9-1-1. The phone rang so many times she was about to hang up.

Finally, a coarse-sounding voice said, "Police. What's your emergency?"

"A burglary in progress." Something clicked as being odd. "Hank? Is that you? Where's the dispatcher?"

"Went home sick. I'm filling in. This sounds like Keira. What's up, girl?"

She might have snapped at his flippancy if she hadn't had more important things on her mind. "I *told* you I'm reporting a breaking and entering. It's at the old mill Douglas owns. The nearest cross street is Oak. Officers on scene requesting backup. Got that?"

"I've got it. A B&E." To her disgust, Hank chuckled. "But it won't do you much good. All our guys are tied up right now. You wouldn't believe the wrecks out on the highway and all the folks who keep seein' boogie men in this fog. We had to call every available man, even those who had the night off."

"The chief is still across the street at the party in the inn," Keira said. "You can reach him there and let him set priorities."

"Me? Leave my post and bother the chief when he's off

duty? You must think I have a death wish. Last I heard, if nobody's dying he doesn't want to be called. Period."

"Fine." Now, she was getting good and steamed. "If you won't take any initiative, I will."

"You do that. In the meantime, I'll radio all units and see if I can shake one loose for you."

"Thanks a heap."

Fingers trembling, Keira began to page through the speed-dial numbers stored in her phone. There it was. Her father's cell. She pushed the button. Listened. And heard the call go to Aiden's voice mail!

"Dad! Dad, pick up. It's Keira. We have a burglary in progress at Douglas's and there are no patrol cars available. If you get this, hurry!"

Her rapid breathing had clouded the car's windows so she wiped a spot to peek through. All she could see was fog and more fog. Using the headlights under those conditions wouldn't help much. Besides, turning them back on might distract Nick.

There was no way to tell what was best. Or where he was at present. Or where the culprit was in relation to her courageous companion.

Keira was growing more and more frantic. She tried phoning her father again with the same result and left another message. If she'd known the number of the inn she could have called there and had him paged. Too bad she hadn't bought one of those fancy new phones that were like tiny computers. If she had those extra features right now, she'd be able to look up any number and call it in seconds.

Only she didn't. She had a department-issued cell that made calls and acted as a pager, period. So much for utilizing the benefits of modern technology.

She turned the ignition key to activate the car's power

windows and rolled them down. Even if she couldn't see she could at least listen.

Surf hitting the rocks along the shore and echoing off the cliffs made a whooshing, roaring sound that ebbed and flowed. Other than that and an occasional car in the distance, the night was silent.

And oh, so dismal.

Keira shivered in spite of her warm wool coat. The salt air weighed heavily on the landscape, lying like a damp, clammy blanket against her skin and making it difficult to draw a satisfying breath.

Wait! Was that scuffling?

She froze, straining to listen. What had she heard? There'd been a dull thud, that was for sure. And now there was another. And breaking wood? Something snapping?

A man cried out!

His voice cut into her heart like a razor. *Nick!* She knew his shout as surely as she knew any. And she couldn't just sit there when he needed help.

Where were those units Hank had notified? And where was her father? Why didn't Douglas bid Merry good-night in a timely manner and come home? *Why, why, why?*

"Please, God," Keira whispered, "tell me what to do."

One hand was still fisted around her father's key ring. Of course! There had to be a jack handle or perhaps even a shotgun in the trunk of the car. She could arm herself and then…

Two figures suddenly emerged from the mist and crashed against the hood. Keira shrieked.

One of the men was Nick. The other was shorter but quite a bit stockier and was using his greater weight to press Nick's body down while they struggled.

The glint of metal told her they were fighting over possession of a handgun. Nick's weapon was blue and this one was more silver-colored so she figured it belonged to the criminal.

Keira grabbed the keys and slid out of the car, hardly noticing when icy slush oozed into her shoes.

"Where's your gun?" she screamed at Nick.

He glanced at her for an instant but didn't reply other than to grunt when his assailant took advantage of the distraction to land a solid punch.

Keira wasn't deterred. She ran to the trunk and tried to unlock it. Why didn't the key fit in the slot? Was her hand shaking too much or was she using the wrong key?

A shadow suddenly loomed.

Nick shouted, "Look out!"

A meaty hand clamped on her wrist, wrested the keys from her and flung them away.

She immediately reverted to her self-defense training and tried to take an appropriate stance. That had been a lot easier to do while wearing more sensible footwear.

The attacker was laughing coarsely and she could smell liquor on his breath as he leaned closer and leered. "Well, well, look what I caught."

Twisting, Keira ignored the pain in her arm and tried to plant the pointed toe of her shoe where it would do the most damage. Her aim was good. The blow landed.

Huffing, cursing, the burly man backhanded her across the face and sent her flying.

She rolled and came up in a fighting stance. A metallic taste on her tongue told her he'd injured her but that wasn't enough to slow her down. Not when she was this ready for battle.

A shot sounded, close enough to make her ears ring, and she instinctively ducked before she realized that the muzzle flash had come from the front of the car where she'd last seen Nick.

Crouching she managed a breathless, "Nick?"

"Yeah. You okay?"

"So far." Keira was peering into the fog, trying to assess the situation. "I don't see him anymore. Did you get him?"

"I don't think so. Stay put. I'm coming to you."

"He has a gun."

"Not anymore. He dropped it over here when he went after you."

"What if he has another one?" She inched closer to the body of the car for cover as Nick joined her.

"Good point. Where's our backup?"

"There weren't any units available. I tried to phone Dad but the call went to voice mail."

"That shot should bring somebody soon. In the meantime, take my gun and sit tight while I see if I can track him down."

"Be careful, okay? I…"

"Keira?"

She could still hear Nick speaking but his voice was beginning to sound distant, as if he were calling to her from atop the lighthouse and she were a ship sailing out of the bay.

The fog around her became an impenetrable curtain. Her lids drifted closed. The blackness was punctuated by brief flashes reminiscent of fireflies, darting and dancing on a warm summer's night.

Her body seemed to be falling gently, like an autumn leaf borne on the wind, rising for a moment, then dipping before finally coming to rest on a soft bed of grass.

A sensation of being cradled persisted.

Totally at peace, Keira surrendered to unconsciousness.

Nick was still sitting on the ground beside the car with Keira in his arms when the first squad car arrived, its siren blaring and lights flashing.

The officers bailed out, drew their guns and stayed low as they approached.

Even with headlights shining in his face, Nick was able to recognize some of the Fitzgeralds.

"She's okay," he announced loudly to allay their fears. "She's starting to come around. I think she just fainted."

Aiden, still in his suit and tie, knelt beside them and took his daughter's hand. "What happened?"

"We surprised a burglar."

"And?" The look in the man's eyes was filled with the fire of a protective parent.

"And," Nick said with equal anger, "I have no doubt it was Anthony Carlton. He was apparently trying to break into my apartment. I told Keira to stay in the car but you know her. She must have decided there was a weapon in the trunk because she got out and tried to open it. That's when he grabbed her."

"Where were you while all this was going on?"

"Picking myself up off the ground. I'd managed to get his gun before he broke away from me. I fired once. The angle was iffy because of the houses across the street so I had to aim high."

"Did you hit him?"

"I doubt it. He didn't flinch but he did take off."

Rising, Aiden barked orders to the group of officers, then spoke into a handheld radio.

Nick only half listened to the chief's report and instructions. All he cared about was the featherlight woman in his arms. Her breathing was steady and strong. So was her pulse.

She stirred. Moaned softly. Nick caressed her cheek, taking care to avoid the redness that was likely to become a bruise. He understood the rage Aiden was feeling. If he'd had Carlton in custody at that moment, the others would probably have had to protect the felon from him instead of the other way around.

"Easy, honey. Take it slow," Nick crooned as Keira's eyelids began to flutter. "I've got you. The cavalry has arrived. We don't have to do anything except sit here for a few minutes while they beat the bushes."

Her eyes widened in fright. "Did he get away?"

Nick nodded. "Yes. But we'll get him. Your dad put out an APB and a full description. There aren't many places around here he can hide. Not for long."

Sighing, she levered herself into a sitting position and tried to smooth her skirt over her skinned knees. "Ouch. Good thing I don't wear nylons often. This pair is ruined. I hope my dress is okay."

"I just hope *you* are. Everything else can be replaced."

"Um." Smiling slightly she winced and touched her cheek. "He walloped me good. I suppose I'll have a bruise."

"Consider it a badge of honor," Nick said. He brushed her bangs off her forehead with his fingertips. "You were amazing."

"I'd have been a lot more impressive if I'd been armed," Keira said. "This is the last time you'll catch me out and about without my gun."

"A holster would have looked a little funny strapped on over that red dress." The urge to kiss her was strong enough that he had difficulty resisting it.

"I don't care. The next fancy outfit I buy is going to have room for a Glock. Maybe two."

"I believe you."

Because she seemed to be getting more and more restless, Nick got to his feet and offered his hand. "Stand up slowly, just in case you're still woozy. You don't want to pass out again."

"I never faint," Keira insisted, although she did take his

hand and continued to hold it. "I must have hit my head when I fell or something."

"Then we need to get you checked. Where's the nearest hospital?"

"Don't be silly. Charles can look me over, at least enough to tell that I'm okay and keep everybody from fussing over me." She glanced toward her father. He and a few of the other officers had gathered in front of the mill. "Did you explain what we saw?"

"Not in detail. I had my hands full when the chief pulled up." He grinned for her benefit. "Not that I'm complaining, mind you. It would have been more fun hugging you if you hadn't been semiconscious at the time, though."

"Yeah, well… Come on. I want to talk to Dad."

"There is one question you haven't asked me yet," Nick said.

"You mean the identity of the guy you were wrestling with? I don't need to. I recognized him from his mug shot. We almost captured Anthony Carlton." Sobering, Keira paused. "I'm sorry he got away because of me."

"Don't take it personally. He got away because he's trained as well or better than you and I are, plus he had the advantage of surprise. We'll get him."

"What do you think he was doing breaking into your apartment?"

"I don't know," Nick said flatly, "but I'm going to find out. I just hope we spotted him on his way *in* instead of on the way out."

"Oh, my, I hadn't thought of that."

"I had. Thank goodness you were a witness. I may need one."

"You think he planted something incriminating inside?"

"It's possible. With him, anything is." Nick quickly recalled details of the dummied-up file before continuing. "He was involved in extortion and drugs back in Boston."

"Then Dad knows that. I wouldn't worry about planted evidence. Even if we do turn up something suspicious, your prints won't be on it. There'll be no question about your innocence."

"Right," Nick said, although he could think of several ways Carlton might try to frame him, including stealing an incriminating item from the Boston P.D.'s evidence locker. All Nick would have had to do was forget to wear gloves one time and his prints would have been left behind.

Had he? When he'd been working undercover, he hadn't been able to glove-up at all. That was the rub. If Carlton had managed to get his hands on something that Nick had touched in the past, something that hadn't been picked up as evidence when the extortion ring had been exposed, it was actually possible that might make him look guilty.

There was only one way to find out. He had to check the apartment himself. And Keira had to be with him to testify to his innocence in case he did spot something odd.

Considering the way she was still holding his hand as if she never intended to let go, it didn't look as if keeping her with him was going to be too difficult.

Getting permission for anything from her father was another matter. If looks could have killed, Aiden's glare when he'd arrived on scene would have already planted Nick as deep as poor Olivia Henry. Or deeper.

"Is it okay if we go in?" Nick asked the chief with attempted nonchalance. He shrugged for emphasis, pretending it didn't matter. "No hurry, of course. I just thought I could tell if anything had been disturbed."

"All right. Go. But my daughter stays out here."

"Sorry, Dad," Keira said with a sweet smile and an exaggerated shiver. "I'm really freezing. I need to get out of this icy fog and it's much warmer inside." The smile spread. "Besides, the whole FBPD is here. I'll be fine."

"It's not the felon I'm worried about," Aiden snapped. He fell into step beside them and Nick could feel his withering gaze as he added, "All right. If you're going in, so am I."

Although Nick would have preferred a few moments alone with Keira, he didn't miss the obvious benefit of having the chief with them. The man might be an overprotective father but he was also a seasoned lawman. Planted evidence would stand out to him the same way it would to Nick. At least, he hoped so.

Opening the apartment door and switching on the lights, Nick spotted several problems immediately. A window had been smashed to gain access so the room was getting chilly. Far worse, there was a bundle of tightly wrapped plastic lying on the kitchen sink in plain sight. It had been slit on one end with a knife that was still sticking out of it. White powder had dribbled onto the counter below the slash.

"That's probably not flour," Nick said, pointing. "And it's not mine."

Beside him he felt Keira's fingers tighten on his. "Of course it isn't."

"We'll bag that and have it examined," the chief said, "and not in Boston. Until I get the lab results back you're relieved of duty, Delfino."

Keira's instant response was almost a shout. *"What?* You can't do that. What happened to 'innocent until proven guilty'?"

The sadness in the chief's expression struck Nick as an omen of worse news. He was right.

"The same goes for you, Officer Fitzgerald. I'm sorry. That's the way it has to be. I can tell you're far too involved in all this to remain impartial. I'll expect your guns and your badges on my desk tomorrow morning."

SEVENTEEN

Nick had one enormous problem—besides the planted drugs. His computer and its carrying case held personal research he'd done on the FBPD. Therefore, if anyone went to the trouble to examine it, his IA division cover would be blown for sure.

Drawing Keira aside he proposed a plan. Her eyebrows shot up as he spoke but she didn't refuse outright.

"You want me to help you break the law?"

"I wouldn't exactly put it that way."

"Oh? Then how would you put it?"

Nick shrugged. "Let's just say it would be expedient if my laptop didn't become part of a long, drawn-out investigation. You can see that, can't you?"

"Why don't you just ask for it?"

"Would you hand it over to a guy you suspected of dealing drugs? No? I didn't think so. But all my pictures from the Henry funeral are on there, plus notes I made that I haven't printed out yet." He paused, letting her think, before he said, "Please?"

"I am going to be in so much trouble if you turn out to be a crook."

"I promise I'm not. Besides, you sort of owe me after keeping Carlton's ID a secret. If I'd known who we were dealing with right away, it might have made a difference."

"How?"

"Well, for one thing I'd have been more on guard."

"Isn't that exactly what you told *me* to do?" Keira asked, faking a pout.

"Yes, and I was right. I just didn't take my own advice seriously enough." His voice lowered and he leaned even closer. "The laptop is in the closet right next to the front door. Do you think you can grab it if I cause enough of a distraction?"

"The question isn't if I can, it's if I will," she said as she began to chew on her lower lip. "There has to be another way."

"Okay, fine," Nick said more loudly. "You stand right here while I go ask."

He was one-hundred-percent sure that the chief would deny his request no matter how rational it sounded. The real question was what Keira would decide to do once she was certain he had made every effort to obtain the computer through proper channels.

"Excuse me, Chief Fitzgerald," he called, crossing the room quickly and placing himself on the opposite side of Aiden so the chief's back was toward the exit. "I was wondering if I might take a few personal items with me since I won't be able to stay here tonight."

"Out of the question," Aiden barked back. "I wouldn't even trust you with your toothbrush at this point."

"Am I free to leave, then? I'll be glad to hang around in case you need me. Whatever you say."

"Go. The less I see of you right now, the better I'll like it."

A surreptitious glance over at Keira gave Nick the impression she was still undecided. Her arms were folded across her chest to hold her coat closed and she looked as if she was shivering. That settled it. His undercover assignment was doomed. The minute the chief checked his laptop he'd learn the truth—and more.

In Nick's opinion, the only plus in the whole mess was that he'd been able to recheck and substantiate a lot of the information the department had provided regarding the Henry murder. His report wasn't quite complete but it did pretty well exonerate the Fitzgerald Bay Police Department. At least there was that in his favor.

Keira turned and led the way out the door as Nick followed. He placed his hand lightly at the small of her back and guided her down the walk to where they'd left her father's car.

"It's all right," Nick said. "I understand. It wasn't fair of me to ask you to do something you felt was wrong."

She turned, made a face and him, said, "*Now* you tell me," and pulled the computer case out from under her coat.

Nick was so shocked he almost dropped it when she shoved it at him. "You did it!"

"Yes, and I don't know why."

"I do." He bent closer and brushed a kiss across her cheek. "You're amazing."

"I'm crazy, that's what I am. Dad is going to be livid if he ever finds out and I'm such a terrible liar he'll probably see the guilt written all over me."

"Just avoid him for a little while longer, then," Nick urged. "I'm going to rent a room at the inn for tonight since I can't go back inside. That way you'll know where to find me."

"I can't believe anybody would buy a stupid frame like this." Shaking her head she glanced back over her shoulder at the condo. "How can my father be so close-minded? He suspended us *both*."

"That's his basic problem," Nick explained sagely. "It's not you and me anymore, Keira, it's *us*. We've become a team and everybody knows it. If I'd been in your dad's shoes, I'd probably have done the same thing."

"It's still wrong."

"Sometimes things aren't clearly black or white. In this case, the chief is just playing it safe." When Nick took a step back she reached for him but he evaded her touch. "Promise me you'll have Charles check your head?"

"I suppose so. Where are you going?"

"I can't stay here with this," he said, tucking the computer case inside his jacket as best he could. "I'll head for the inn. It's not far. I can walk."

"What if Carlton is out there in the fog waiting to pounce?"

"Chances of that are pretty slim," Nick assured her. "And you'll be safe enough with all these cops around. Tell the chief where I'm headed and then see if Charles will make a house call to check you over. I still don't like the fact that you passed out."

"Okay." Keira's voice drifted after him as he strode off. "Be careful."

He waved without turning around. She was right about the chances of an ambush while he was on foot. Nick would like nothing better than to have another opportunity to face and capture his sworn enemy.

And while he was at it, to avenge Keira for the bruise on her cheek. When he'd seen her go down...

Nick's stomach clenched. If anything had happened to Keira he'd have never forgiven himself. Imagining it had been bad enough.

Thinking back, he realized that for the second time in his life, he had almost prayed.

That would never happen, of course. He'd been able to handle plenty of crises by himself in the past and nothing had changed since then. He was ready for whatever Carlton or any other criminal dished out.

Now that he'd turned a corner, he let the leather case swing in time with his strides. Aiden's actions regarding the planted evidence were one more step toward total exoneration. When he had suspended Keira, he had gone a long way toward proving he ran a clean department. Coupled with the results of the interviews Nick had already conducted and the conversations he'd overheard, he knew he was going to be able to officially clear the FBPD of any wrongdoing.

He pictured Keira's lovely face once again and a familiar twinge of guilt and regret hit him. He'd have to face her, of course. Tell her everything himself rather than merely confess to the chief and then leave town. He owed her that much. And more. But it was going to be the most difficult thing he'd ever had to do.

As Nick saw it, the only advantage would be that if he left, Anthony Carlton would undoubtedly follow him. It was almost worth it to know Keira and the others would then be safer.

Now, if he only knew who had murdered Olivia Henry he'd have all the loose ends tied up.

Yeah. As long as you didn't count what this entire assignment had done to his heart and soul, he added, sobering.

Stepping up onto the porch of the inn, he stomped his feet on the mat, then sighed deeply and went inside.

"Look straight at me," Charles told Keira. "I want to check the reactions of your pupils."

"I know that. We had to take an advanced first-aid course at the academy." She grimaced and felt the tenderness of her bruised cheek. "I'm fine, okay? I only called you because I'd promised Nick."

"I know," the doctor said with a lopsided smile. "He phoned me, too."

"He didn't trust me?"

"Now, don't go getting irate. He was just worried about you and wanted to make sure I was available tonight. I'd have been here sooner but I had to get an emergency sitter for the twins."

"You woke Irene? Oh, dear. She needs her rest. She gets up so early every morning."

Her brother laughed. "I didn't call Irene. As a matter of fact, Dad was available to watch the kids as soon as he'd sealed up Nick's apartment."

"So, you heard what happened?"

"Yes. Sounds like you had a rough evening."

"The first part was fine. It just didn't end well." She shivered. "Right now I could use a cup of that special hot cocoa Dad used to fix us."

Charles chuckled. "I had to make him promise not to wake up my kids to feed that to them."

"He probably did it, anyway. He does love children."

"Good thing, since he had so many."

"Yes, but since I was the last, I guess I cured them."

"Or they figured they could never do better."

"Thanks." She blinked to focus after the brightness of his penlight had made spots dance in front of her eyes. "My head feels okay but the side of my face is pretty sore. Think I'll have a shiner?"

"Probably. Are you looking forward to it?"

"Maybe a little. It's a badge of honor. Of course, it would count for more if I had actually won the fight."

"Unarmed and against a man twice your size?"

"Hey, it's possible. Not probable but possible. I would have done better if I hadn't been wearing those stupid fancy shoes. I'm sorry I missed my chance to stomp him with one of my spiked heels."

"Probably just as well. Dad showed me a picture of Carlton. He's a nasty-looking character."

"He smelled worse than he looked, tonight. I could tell he'd been drinking, which may be why I was able to land a good kick. I imagine his reflexes were hampered."

"Does your head hurt right now?"

"No. Any idea why I keeled over? I'd hate to make a practice of it."

"It could have been because of low blood sugar. When was the last time you ate?"

"Hmm. Lunch, maybe. I had a couple sips of punch at the Valentine's party but I couldn't eat a bite."

"Too nervous?"

"Maybe." Watching her big brother's kind eyes, she suspected that he understood, although if she were seeking a family confidant she'd rather it be Fiona.

"Be careful," Charles warned. "There's something about Delfino that bothers me."

Keira chuckled wryly. "Funny. He said the same thing about you."

"That's *not* funny. At least not lately." Gathering up his medical equipment, he started to pull on his jacket. "It's bad enough that folks like Burke Hennessy keep bad-mouthing me. My income really dropped off, too."

"Then don't forget to charge us for this house call," Keira reminded him, hoping the teasing would help lift his spirits. "And remember what Pastor Larch said. 'This, too, shall pass.'"

"The sooner the better."

Keira noticed that his usual slight limp seemed more exaggerated as he crossed to the door, probably because he was overtired. She hated that he'd been wounded but considering what might have happened to him while he was serving overseas, he'd probably gotten off easy.

"Lock this door behind me," Charles ordered. "I'll send Dad right home so you won't be alone for long."

"I'm not afraid. Besides, Irene's here."

"A lot of good she'd be if somebody tried to break in," her brother said.

"Nobody's going to break in. Carlton was out to get Nick, not me. I'm going to lock up, then go take a long, hot shower to soothe my sore muscles."

"You're sure there's no more dizziness?"

"None. Not a smidgen. Now that I'm barefoot my equilibrium is perfect. I don't know how any woman can stand wearing those torturous high heels all the time."

Judging by the flash of pain that crossed his face for an instant, Keira assumed her careless reference to fashion had caused him to think of Kathleen, his former wife. The family tended to agree that the woman's departure from Fitzgerald Bay in search of the romantic life of an artist was for the best. It had just been hard to watch poor Charles suffer after she'd deserted him. He'd been alone since shortly after the twins' birth.

For a time, a few members of the family had wondered if nanny Olivia Henry might eventually fill that void in his life but, sadly, that was not to be.

Keira reached out and gave her brother a hug as he was leaving. "Thanks for coming by. I was afraid Nick was going to insist they throw me into an ambulance and head for the nearest E.R. I think he might have if you hadn't been so handy."

"Glad to be of service. I'll phone you in the morning. In the meantime, it wouldn't hurt to stay awake a few more hours for safety's sake. If you have any strange symptoms or feel even a little bit sick, call me immediately. Day or night. Got that?"

"Yes, sir."

In parting, she gave him the same kind of silly salute she

usually reserved for their father and was rewarded with a snappy marine salute in return.

Keira closed the door, locked it and leaned against it. If the time ever came for her to choose a mate, she planned to choose more wisely than Charles had. She wanted a marriage like the one her parents had enjoyed, or like Fiona and Jimmy had shared. There was happiness to be found out there in the world. All she had to do was avoid making any huge mistakes.

Her ensuing thoughts immediately focused on Nick Delfino. That man was as hardheaded as she was. It would probably be difficult for them to get along while sharing the same profession, yet there was something special about him that intrigued her.

She knew—she just knew—if she delved deep enough, she would find out he was even more perfect than she already believed.

And, as soon as her father was through with his silly investigation of the package of narcotics Carlton had planted in Nick's apartment, she was going to insist he apologize for ever doubting Nick's innocence.

The hot shower had refreshed Keira. The bologna sandwich on wheat bread she'd wolfed down hadn't hurt, either.

Aiden had checked on her when he'd come home but he hadn't tried to chat before bidding her a terse good-night.

Keira wasn't any more eager to talk to him than he'd been to face her. She figured he'd made himself scarce because he'd been worried that she'd start another argument or try to continue their previous one. She had no such plans. Not yet, anyway.

If she was going to argue, she needed to have all the facts and be on firm ground first. The best way she could think of doing that, without actually visiting the station, was via the internet. Police records might not be open to her without proper authorization but nothing said she couldn't search newspaper archives. In a way, Nick had given her that idea when he'd asked her to grab his laptop.

A sweatshirt over matching pants kept her cozy. Legs crossed, she sat on her bed with her laptop open in front of her. The first thing she did was check emails in case one of her siblings had sent news of Carlton's capture. Sadly, there was no such message.

Clicking on her favorites list, she located the Boston newspapers, then did an archive search using Carlton's name.

There was plenty of information to choose from. Keira scanned a few of the most recent articles, then decided to skip the rest of those in favor of checking farther back.

That was when the search got really interesting.

Her eyes narrowed as she peered at the screen, paging down quickly, then backtracking to soak up more details. There was a photo of Carlton looking as mean as ever. He was in cuffs and being hauled off to jail by several officers whose faces were not familiar.

In the back of the shot, however, a man in street clothes hid his face behind a folded newspaper while a reporter shoved a microphone at him.

Keira clicked on a smaller picture that led to a video and turned up the volume while it loaded.

"We're here on Boston Common reporting on an undercover sting operation involving some of the city's finest," the newsman said. "I'm speaking with a lieutenant from the Internal Affairs Division who prefers to remain anonymous. Tell us, Lieutenant. How were you able to infiltrate the gang of fellow officers without making them suspicious?"

The moment the officer spoke, Keira knew it was Nick. She listened as the love of her life briefly explained how Internal Affairs operated. When he cited his long history of cooperation with the State Police she realized why her father and brothers had felt so uneasy around him.

Her brain was spinning, her thoughts so conflicted she wondered if she should call Charles and tell him she was experiencing immense confusion. Outing crooked cops was good, right? Somebody had to do it.

But that didn't explain what an IA man was doing in Fitzgerald Bay. No matter how many times Keira tried to banish the painful conclusion, it kept coming back to haunt her. As she whispered the truth, she realized that everything now made perfect sense. "He's not here to solve the murder—he's investigating *us*."

Nick was plying his specialty among the members of the local force. He'd been sent to break them, to ruin them, to prove that Charles was guilty and that her family had been sheltering him. That had to be the truth. It was too logical to be a product of her imagination. And it explained so much that had puzzled her before.

He had fooled even her father. Aiden apparently thought Nick's temporary assignment had been made as a favor to him rather than the double-cross it really was. How hurt he was going to be when he realized one or more of his supposed friends in high places had betrayed his trust.

Keira grasped her knees and curled up, staring at the walls of her bedroom and seeing nothing. Nothing but Nick. And the fading of her pretty dreams for their future.

Nick had had to accept a smaller room at the Sugar Plum Inn this time but he didn't care. He slammed a fist into his other cupped hand and paced. In retrospect, he assumed Carlton had been behind everything, beginning with the first break-in, although it was still possible that some of the most minor incidents had originated with a different antagonist. One thing was certain. It was Carlton who had tried to bury him and Keira on the beach. And Carlton who had smacked her so hard she was going to carry the bruise for weeks.

So angry he could hardly contain himself, Nick kept pounding his fist into his hand and fighting for self-control. The guy had hurt his Keira.

"No. Not *my* Keira. Not anymore," he muttered. "As if she ever was."

There must be some way out of this, something he could do to salvage their relationship. There had to be. So why couldn't he think of it?

Pausing as he passed the small, west-facing window, he looked out. Fog still drifted in layers over the town and plaintive moans echoed from ships off the coast as they repeatedly blew long warning blasts on their horns.

One slender object, lighted from below, pierced through the fog enough to be recognizable. Because the ground rose as it left the shore, the church steeple was visible above the mist.

Nick stared. Wondered for a moment. "No. That's ridiculous," he whispered to himself. There was no help to be had from that quarter. Never had been, never would be.

He turned away and resumed his pacing.

EIGHTEEN

There were several ways Keira coped with life's disappointments. One was to go for a run along the shoreline but that was only fun in warmer weather. The other was to grab a big spoon and a carton of chocolate ice cream. This was certainly the perfect night for it.

Padding barefoot into the dark kitchen, she went straight to the upright freezer, opening the adjoining refrigerator to let out just enough light to see by. "Hmm. Decisions, decisions, decisions."

She didn't really want ice cream any more than she'd wanted the treats at Victoria's party but she had to fill the void in her heart with something, and chocolate would have to do.

What about tomorrow? Keira wondered. That was a whole other problem, wasn't it? Since she and Nick had both been relieved of duty, she supposed that would act as a buffer. The first thing she intended to do was try to catch her father before he left the house in the morning and make him watch the video she'd stumbled on.

"Funny," Keira said with a sigh. "If that Carlton guy hadn't shown up in town, I probably wouldn't have figured this out before making a worse fool of myself."

Sighing, she opened the ice-cream carton and wiggled

her spoon to work it into the firm contents. How ironic. A dangerous fugitive was the reason she finally knew the truth about her partner. If *that* was God's answer to her prayer regarding Nick, she was certainly not thrilled.

Spoon and treat in hand, Keira started out of the kitchen. A noise behind her made her pause.

"Dad? Is that you?"

No one answered. "Dad?" To her shame there was a quaver of fear in her voice this time. And still no reply.

Knowing the layout of the kitchen, Keira began to assess her chances of escape. It wasn't totally dark in the house. Not the way it would have been if the fog had been thicker and had totally blotted out the moonlight.

Moreover, this was her home. She knew every inch of it. That gave her a home-field advantage.

Ice cream in one hand, spoon in the other, she wondered which would make the best weapon until she could reach her shoulder bag and grab her cell phone or improvise otherwise.

Probably the hard lump of frozen dessert, although she supposed she could always poke an attacker in the eye with the spoon if she couldn't get to a gun.

Picturing such a battle almost made her laugh. Intense nervousness often did that. So did embarrassment. So did a lot of circumstances if she were honest with herself.

She turned the spoon around and slid the cuff of her sweatshirt over its bowl. The filigreed silver handle was a poor excuse for a knife but it would have to do.

"I'm armed," Keira announced boldly, her arm extended in a defensive pose. "If you leave quietly I'll let you go."

The ensuing silence almost convinced her that she had imagined a prowler until she sniffed. Something smelled odd. Liquor. And sweat. He was here!

Edging backward toward the door to the hallway in search of her purse, Keira tried to decide where her erstwhile attacker might be lurking. The room was enormous. And neat. And provided few places where a big man like Anthony Carlton could hide.

So where…?

A meaty hand clamped over her mouth before she had a chance to scream. The spoon clattered to the floor and the carton of ice cream slipped from her grasp when she tried to pitch it over her shoulder at his head.

His laugh was low, sinister. "You were a lot prettier in that dress you had on before."

Struggling, Keira wished she was still wearing the matching red shoes because he was in the perfect place for an arch stomp. She tried to harm him with her bare heel but all she succeeded in doing was hurting her own foot as it scraped against the metal-rimmed laces of his boot.

If her father awoke and came to investigate, he'd probably be armed. If Irene Mulrooney was the one who stumbled upon this scene, however, the older woman could easily be hurt—or even killed.

Keira decided she must not let that happen. Forcing herself to relax and stop struggling, she felt her captor's grip loosen.

"Now you're being smart," Carlton whispered near her ear.

The odor of his breath almost made her gag but she managed to nod.

"Not a peep. You hear?"

Another nod and the hand was no longer covering her face. "What—what do you want?"

"Well, not you, pretty lady, although if you still had that red dress on I might change my mind." He chortled quietly. "For a cop you're sure dumb. I guess that comes from being a rookie."

Grabbing a fistful of her sweatshirt at the shoulder, he shoved her shoulder bag at her. "Get your phone and give it to me."

"What if I don't…?"

"Don't mess with me, lady," Carlton growled. As soon as he had the phone in hand, he cast the bag aside and propelled her toward the back door. "Let's go."

"Where are you taking me?"

"What do you care?" the fugitive said wryly. "Maybe we'll take in the sights from the top of the lighthouse. How does that sound?"

"But, why me?"

His resulting laugh made her skin crawl. "Because I need you for bait, darlin'. I'm going fishing."

Nick's cell rang. He glanced at his watch. Who would be calling at this time of the morning?

He looked at the ID number. *Keira? Now? Why?*

Instead of hello he answered with, "What's wrong," and heard a menacing laugh.

"Nice of your girlfriend to put you on speed dial. Makes it much easier for me."

"Carlton." Nick was gripping his phone so tightly his fingers started to tingle.

"That's me, buddy. Sorry I couldn't hang around and chat earlier. I had an appointment with a real pretty lady cop."

"If you hurt her…"

"Nothing's gonna happen to the rookie. I haven't got anything against her except the uniform she wears. Now, you, that's a different story."

"What do you want?" Nick asked, already assuming there was a trade offer coming, one he would gladly accept.

"You know what. I want you. Alone. You can take her place and we'll have a nice little reunion."

"Fine. Where?"

Nick was throwing clothing onto the bed while he talked.

When he heard his nemesis say, "The lighthouse," he froze. "What are you talking about?"

"You heard me. I'll meet you in half an hour at the top of the lighthouse. And come alone. I'll be able to see everything from up there so don't try anything funny. Understand?"

"Yeah. I understand."

The phone went dead before Nick had a chance to ask to speak to Keira. Carlton might have merely stolen her cell. Maybe she was still safe at home.

And maybe her father was going to kill him himself if she wasn't, Nick added as he dressed. Aiden's house was where he was going first.

And if Keira's not there? he asked himself.

Then it would be time for a full confession. He just hoped it wasn't going to be too little, too late.

Keira's feet and hands were so cold they stung. Her teeth chattered. Her body shook. Every step sent needles of pain shooting up her legs.

As her captor dragged her through the side yard of the Fitzgerald house and pushed her into his old pickup truck, she was almost glad. At least that meant she was no longer forced to walk barefoot across snow and refrozen slush.

Pulling up her legs under her, she tried to slip her feet inside the cuffs of her sweatpants. That helped a little. So did pulling down the long sleeves over her hands. It wasn't as good as having gloves and boots but considering the gravity of her current situation, she figured she'd be doing well to survive, let alone find a modicum of comfort.

Carlton slid behind the wheel and released the parking brake. He left the headlights and engine off until they had coasted down the hill a short way, then fired up the truck and hit the gas.

It occurred to Keira to ask if he was trying to kill them

both by racing so recklessly through the fog but she held her tongue. The less attention she called to herself, the better.

From what she'd read in the newspaper archives about this man, he tended to be unforgiving and brutal. That was how he'd escaped from custody in the first place. Some of his fellow officers had treated him kindly and he'd repaid them by grabbing a gun, shooting up the station and fleeing.

According to ensuing reports, he had later murdered one of the dirty cops who had been going to testify against him in exchange for a reduced sentence. No wonder Nick had been so concerned when he'd learned that Carlton was nearby.

Confounded by her musings, Keira lowered her forehead to her knees and pulled herself into a ball on the truck seat, arms wrapped around her calves. If Nick had known how dangerous the man was, why hadn't he warned her?

Because he didn't know Carlton was here. We didn't tell him about the fingerprint ID, she answered. If Nick had suspected that an actual threat was imminent, he surely would have spoken up and admitted everything. She knew he would have.

And if I had confided in him, as my partner, I wouldn't be in this fix now, either.

Keira's jaw clenched. Whether or not that conclusion was true, she intended to cling to it. To believe Nick would have told the truth in order to protect her.

The truck skidded around a corner and bumped over a curb. She had to brace herself to keep from sliding off the seat. The cylindrical side of the familiar white tower of the lighthouse loomed ahead.

There were no lights on at Charles's nearby home. Everything was dark as a tomb.

Bad analogy, Keira thought wryly. *Really, really bad.*

Nick had phoned Aiden to alert him that he'd be arriving and to ask that the other Fitzgerald officers be included in their emergency meeting. Rather than wait for a ride, he'd jogged the two blocks up the hill and managed to beat Ryan and Owen. They slid their cars into the driveway just as Nick was running onto the porch.

He didn't have to knock. Aiden jerked open the door and dragged him inside by the sleeve of his jacket while the others brought up the rear.

"Where's my daughter?"

"That's what I came here to talk about." Breathing hard, Nick led the way into the living room. Judging by the dirty looks he was getting, he wouldn't be given long to explain before the group lost its collective patience.

Nick faced Aiden. "You've checked the house like I said? She's not here?"

"All I found was some melting ice cream on the floor in the kitchen. Her bed hasn't been slept in. It looked like she'd been sitting on it and using her computer."

"All right. Then I know where she is and who took her."

In the background he heard a female gasp and spotted the housekeeper entering with a steaming coffeepot and a tray of mugs. "I can't believe I slept through it all," Irene said. "I'm so sorry, Aiden."

"Just put that down and leave us," the chief ordered. He waited until the men were alone again before he glared at Nick and said, "Okay. We're waiting. Where's Keira?"

"Carlton has her," Nick said, feeling the words nearly choking him. "He wants me to trade myself for her."

"Where?"

"The lighthouse."

"When?"

Nick checked his watch. "He gave me half an hour. We have fifteen minutes left."

"Why my daughter?" Aiden asked.

"Two reasons, I suspect," Nick replied. "One, he wants to

hurt me and he knows how much I care about her. Two, she's an honest cop. He hates them almost as much as he hates me."

"Because of something that happened in Boston?"

"Yes." Nodding, Nick briefly explained his former job before he said, "I didn't come here just to help you solve the Henry murder. I was sent to Fitzgerald Bay to prove that you and your department were falsifying evidence in an attempt to exonerate Charles." He cleared his throat. "The reason you couldn't find much in my file was because it had been scrubbed to hide my real background."

The murderous glares coming his way didn't surprise Nick. He did, however, have one more thing to say. "If you had told me up front that you'd lifted Carlton's prints, we might have avoided all this, you know."

Aiden grimaced. "I know. Keira wanted to but I didn't trust you. And I was right."

"It was my job," Nick countered. "You'll be glad to hear I didn't find any indication that you were being untruthful."

"That's little consolation right now," the chief said. He looked to his sons. "We'll have to be very careful how we go about this. Charles's place will make a perfect command post. I'll call and let him know we're coming."

He handed Nick his spare key ring. "You take my car and stage in front of the police station. We'll work our way into the house by the back way and radio when we're ready. Come in hot and loud to cover any movements we'll be making as we get into position."

"All right." Nick fisted the keys. "He said he wanted just me so I'll have to make the climb to the top alone."

"I know." Slowly, deliberately, Aiden offered his hand.

Nick shook it, assuming the other man was about to wish him good luck. He was floored when the chief said, "Godspeed. We'll all be praying for you."

* * *

"C-can't we just wait here in the truck?" Keira stammered through chattering teeth. "I'm freezing."

"Too bad. I need to be high enough to see if your boyfriend tries to pull another fast one."

"What can he possibly do?" She had a few ideas of her own but they involved other members of her family as backup. Her fondest hope was that Nick had disobeyed Carlton's orders and had asked for their help.

"Plenty," he grumbled, dragging her across the truck's seat and pulling her out the driver's door after him. "But he won't win this time. Not while I've got you."

"We know you pushed that boulder down on us," she said, stumbling and struggling as he tugged her along. "What about the other stuff? Was it you who tried to run me down?"

"What if it was?"

"I—I just wondered how long you'd been in town, that's all. Why didn't you plant the narcotics when you ransacked Nick's room at the inn?"

He guffawed, keeping the sound muffled enough that it didn't carry well. "How far back are you planning to go? Would you like to blame that old murder on me, too? Huh? Well, forget it. I was in Boston until a week ago."

"But you did hit my patrol car. I recognize this truck."

"Maybe. I almost took a shot at you and my buddy Delfino outside that big party at the inn, too, but there were too many witnesses milling around. I might not have gotten away with it."

"So you went to Nick's and planted the dope, instead?"

"You're a nosy little thing, aren't you?"

"I'd just like to know how you managed to stay hidden and accomplish so much when everybody in Fitzgerald Bay knows everybody else."

"Because I'm smarter than all of you put together," Carlton

boasted. "I moved into an empty house practically across the street from the old mill, hid out and kept a low profile while I watched Delfino and everybody else come and go. Made me laugh to see how clueless you all were."

"The Smith place. Of course. We didn't search it because the truck that was parked there wasn't the same one that tried to run me down."

"You sure about that?" Chortling, he slammed her against the door at the base of the lighthouse and ordered, "Open it."

"I can't. It's locked."

Carlton snorted derisively. "You must think I'm dumber than your partner." He reached past her and twisted the knob easily. "I already made sure we could get in."

Rusty hinges creaked. Keira was unceremoniously shoved inside and the door slammed behind her.

"Climb," the burly man ordered. He poked her in the ribs with the barrel of his gun. "And don't stop until we get to the catwalk at the top."

NINETEEN

Nick's heart was in his throat. It was all he could do to sit there in the chief's private car and wait for the order to move in. The radio in his hand felt as if it weighed a hundred pounds and his heart was hammering so loudly he wondered if he'd be able to hear anything over the noise of his own pulse.

Finally, the radio crackled. All Aiden said was, "Go."

That made sense considering the fact that Carlton might also have a police radio and be listening to their calls. Hopefully, that was not the case because Nick needed all the help he could get and the situation would probably come out a lot better if their enemy didn't know what they were up to.

Not that Nick did. Not really. All he knew was that he was the decoy. What actions the others took was up to them.

In truth, he didn't care what happened as long as he got Keira out in one piece. One living, breathing piece.

He revved the engine and dropped the transmission into gear. Hands fisted on the wheel, he gritted his teeth. This plan had to work. Had to be successful. The alternative was unacceptable.

Ahead, the fog seemed to part momentarily, almost as if he were meant to make the short trip safely and quickly. Was this kind of thing what Aiden had meant when he'd said they'd pray? He doubted it.

If there was even the slightest chance that God might help Keira, Nick figured he'd better ask. Only how? He hadn't been raised in church and the prayers he had heard a few times had sounded formal and very proper.

"That's not me," Nick said aloud. "I'm just a regular guy who happens to be in love with a woman who needs Your help right now, Lord. I don't deserve anything from You. But she does. So help her, will You? Please, God? And if it'll do any good, use me. I'm not much but I'm all Yours."

The sky didn't open. But Nick did feel a strange sort of peace. And an added strength of purpose.

As he wheeled the car into the parking lot at the base of the old lighthouse, he made sure the tires squealed, then revved the engine again before shutting it off. If that wasn't enough distraction for the cops he hoped were already on scene, there was nothing he could do about it.

Not wanting to give away their plan due to inopportune radio traffic, he laid the handheld unit on the seat of the car and got out without it. He was on his own now. It was just him and Carlton.

And the Lord? Perhaps. Time would tell. As far as Nick was concerned, it was all well and good to turn to prayer if a person had no other choice. In his case, he'd start by relying on his gun and his wits. They were proven weapons. The spiritual stuff was not.

Out of breath, her legs aching, her feet feeling as though icicles as sharp as needles were piercing them, Keira stumbled the final few steps to the top level of the tower and fell to her knees.

Here was where the giant light had once glowed, guiding mariners through treacherous shoals and into the safety of the bay. Now that global positioning satellites had taken over and the lights were no longer needed, a few, like this one, had been preserved as historical sites.

She couldn't imagine having to climb those spiral stairs, night after night, to tend to the light and keep it burning, not even after the original open flame had been converted to electricity. Right now, she actually wished the light was in use so it would provide a little warmth. The next time she got up at night to raid the fridge, she was definitely going to remember to wear slippers.

She shivered and wrapped her arms around herself. *If there ever is another night like this.* Hopefully, her days of being dragged from her warm home and forced to endure such biting cold would be over as soon as Nick rescued her.

Nick Delfino. Here I go again, she mused, *thinking of* him. Dreaming of him as if he were her knight in shining armor. More like dented, rusty, squeaky armor, she corrected, still miffed yet nevertheless yearning to see him again. What was wrong with her? Didn't she have the sense of a clam? Apparently not.

Keira sighed and closed her eyes, half picturing Nick, half praying for him—and for herself. Her personal faith had been a lot stronger when she was younger. These days she was more apt to try to figure things out and fix them herself than to take her problems straight to the Lord the way she used to. The loss of her mother had been the turning point. She'd prayed her heart out and Mama had still died.

Was it going to be her turn tonight? she wondered. Or maybe Nick's?

"Please, Lord, no," she whispered behind her hands so her captor wouldn't overhear. "Not Nick. Please, not Nick."

Because I love him, she added silently. In spite of all his lies, all his undercover prying regarding the FBPD, she was deeply, desperately in love with him.

She just hoped and prayed they would both live long enough for her to have a chance to tell him how she felt.

Right now, their future wasn't looking very promising.

"Carlton!" Nick cupped both hands around his mouth and shouted from the base of the tower.

"Come on up" echoed down.

There was no doubt in Nick's mind that he was about to face an ominous foe. If circumstances had not included Keira, he would never have agreed to this risky meeting.

Aiden, Ryan, Owen and Douglas must be close by. At least Nick hoped they were. If he was truly about to enter the lion's den, he'd much rather have backup.

As he put his foot on the bottom step and started to climb, it occurred to him that the reference to a lion's den was biblical. Funny he'd remember that right now.

Nick paused halfway up, listening, then shouted. "I want to know Keira's okay." *And make sure you really have her,* he added to himself.

"Fine."

He heard scuffling from above and a tiny squeal before she said, "Ouch! Okay, okay. I'll talk to him."

"Keira? Are you all right?"

"Yes. I'm sorry, Nick. I should have been more careful."

"Don't worry. I'm coming on up."

"No! Don't do it. He's got a gun again."

Nick heard Carlton's maniacal laugh and sensed that the man was teetering on the edge of insanity. "Let the woman go. She can pass me on the stairs."

"You must think I'm dumber than dirt," the fugitive said with a snort. "Keep climbing, Delfino. We'll talk when I can look you in the eye."

The final few steps were the hardest. Nick was afraid Carlton would shoot him the moment he poked his head through to the metal catwalk that circled the uppermost level.

Instead, fog-filtered moonlight showed that the man was using Keira as a human shield, apparently anticipating the same kind of lethal welcome. Her eyes were wide, her face flushed, and she was grasping the arm that imprisoned her with both her hands.

At that moment, it was all Nick could do to stifle the urge to launch an attack, even though taking a bullet was a fool's choice. Logic prevailed. A lot of good he'd be to Keira if he was lying there bleeding to death.

"Okay. You have me. Now let her go," Nick said. He extended his arms, hands open, to demonstrate his desire for peace.

"Take out your gun and toss it over the side," Carlton ordered. "Now."

There was no way to fake a throw. His foe would be able to tell if the gun didn't actually fall. Not only were they standing on an open metal grate, the glistening railing around the catwalk was no more than a single bar of ice-coated pipe that stood about waist high.

"All right." He slid his Glock from its holster at the small of his back and displayed it before flinging it over the side. It clattered on the rocks below. Then, everything was silent except for the whooshing of the surf and the whistle of the increasing wind off the Atlantic.

"Now the other one," Carlton ordered. "Every good cop has a holdout gun on him."

"Not tonight," Nick replied. "I left in too big a hurry."

"Pull up your pant legs. Both of them. Show me."

As Nick bent forward to comply, he cast a wary glance at Keira and noticed a glimmer in her eyes that worried him. Surely she didn't intend to try to overpower a man the size of the one who had his forearm pressed across her neck and shoulders. She'd never be able to toss him unless he was moving, and even then it was iffy.

Keira nodded.

Nick shook his head and stared, willing her to obey.

Carlton didn't seem to be paying attention to anything except Nick's lower legs, apparently expecting to see a second holster or knife sheath.

From his bent-over position, Nick saw both of Keira's bare feet lift off the catwalk at the same time. She was going to do it. The crazy, brave, impossible woman was going to try to unbalance her captor. Didn't she realize that a trained officer would be expecting a move like that?

Nick had two choices. He could wait for a possible opening later or try to take advantage of Keira's efforts right now. Even if she wasn't totally successful she might distract Carlton. Maybe that would be enough.

Her feet came down. Her upper body arched. Although the heavyset man did shift to a wider stance he didn't fly over her head the way the self-defense manuals illustrated.

Nevertheless, his attention was momentarily diverted. That was all Nick needed. Already crouching, he dived for Carlton's knees and tackled him like a football player.

Everyone went down.

Keira screamed.

Nick shouted.

A shot went wild as Carlton hit the catwalk and Nick began to grapple with him.

Staccato thudding began in the distance. It sounded as if a herd of cattle was stampeding up the stairs.

Nick briefly caught sight of Keira. She was moving, crawling, hopefully taking herself out of the fray.

Then, to his horror she got to her feet and threw herself on top of their attacker!

* * *

Numb from the cold, Keira didn't stop to wonder where she was getting the strength to act. She only knew she must do something, anything, to help Nick. Carlton had him pinned to the metal catwalk grid and was beating him silly. She didn't know how much more punishment he could take without passing out. If that happened, he was sure to be thrown to his death on the rocks below.

In the back of her mind, she did realize that she faced the same possible fate. That didn't stop her. She hit Carlton with a full body slam and wound both arms around his neck in a choke hold.

He began to swing his hands behind him as if trying to swat a pesky fly.

Keira hung tight. She heard someone screaming like a banshee. It was *her!*

The shoulders on which she lay rose up. Her world tilted. As Carlton rolled off Nick, she felt her back being pressed hard against the icy, slippery, metal flooring grate.

Kicking, she tried to land a blow, any blow, anywhere on her opponent's body as he turned to face her. It was no use. His much greater bulk had her pinned. Helpless.

What about Nick? Was he free now? Was he okay? Had she at least succeeded in helping him?

Tossing her head from side to side as she struggled to escape, she caught a glimpse of Nick. He was stirring. Barely. And still lying beside them.

Keira smelled her attacker's breath, fetid and warm in her face. She snapped up her head as hard and as fast as she could. Her forehead caught him in the nose. She heard a sickening crack.

An instant later Carlton began to bellow unintelligibly.

She didn't care that her own head was throbbing. At least she'd finally landed a useful blow.

The hefty man levered himself off her. He was cupping his face while blood poured from the space between his fingers. "You little…"

Stunned herself, Keira flipped over and tried to crawl away.

He grabbed for her bare ankle. His hand was slick. She jerked free for an instant before he clamped her more tightly.

Reaching for Nick, she saw his look of horror. He fisted a handful of her sweatshirt as she was being dragged away from him.

Keira screamed, loud and long.

She kicked as if swimming against a deadly riptide, hoping and praying she'd land at least a few useful blows and wishing for the hundredth time that she'd thought to wear shoes.

There was no time to reason. No time to pray. No time to do anything but live or die.

Nick's vision wasn't clear enough to make out a lot of details. That didn't matter. He was lucid enough to tell precisely what was happening. The tableau unfolded as if in slow motion.

Carlton rose up. Keira kept kicking at him. He staggered. Started to slip.

Maybe Carlton lost his footing because of the blood from his broken nose, maybe because of the wetness and icy coating the fog had left behind. Nick didn't know. All he was sure of was that the man was teetering on the brink of a fall and he still had hold of Keira. They both did.

"Grab the edge!" Nick shouted to her. "Don't let him pull you over!"

A shorter man might have been able to lean against the narrow railing and save himself. Carlton was too top-heavy and too off-balance for that. The instant he released his hold on Keira's ankle to reach for a more solid handhold, he fell.

The scream was short-lived, ending with a thud that was punctuated by a sickening cracking sound.

For a heartbeat Nick thought Keira had fallen, too. Then he saw her fingers curled around the slippery metal edge of the flooring grid.

He lunged. Grabbed her wrist and held on as tightly as he could.

"Niiiiick!" she screeched.

"I've got you. Hang on."

"My fingers. They're so cold. I can't feel them."

Lying prone he found her other wrist and clamped on to it, too. He knew if he tried to stand and gain the leverage to lift her, there was a chance he'd lose his tenuous hold.

Yet if he lay there for too much longer, his grip might fail. So might hers. The result would be the same.

Please, God, help us, Nick prayed, meaning every word, believing beyond anything he'd ever experienced before. He didn't see how they were going to get out of this alive but for once he realized he didn't have to know. He simply had to trust. One thing was certain. He'd go over the edge with her before he'd let go.

Shouts behind them caught his attention. So did Keira's whimpering call of, "Daddy?"

Nick felt strong hands covering his, helping him hoist his treasure.

Three men drew Keira back onto the catwalk, then assisted Nick. The moment he was seated in safety, she threw herself into his arms.

Nobody had to urge Nick to embrace her. He simply held her close while they both trembled. He knew Keira was weeping. He just hoped no one noticed that his eyes were moist, too.

The parking lot was aglow with the lights of emergency vehicles and patrol cars by the time Keira and Nick were guided to the base of the tower.

When someone draped a blanket around her shoulders, she wished she were sharing it with Nick. Ryan and Owen had led him off while she was taken to be checked over by EMTs and her doctor brother.

"Except for some hypothermia, they say you're in pretty good shape," Charles pronounced as the ambulance crew completed a cursory examination.

She touched his hand. "Then where's Nick? I want to see Nick."

"He'll be back as soon as Dad questions him."

"Not with his nightstick, I hope. Nick saved my life up there." She made a face. "He's IA. I discovered it when I was doing a computer search."

Her brother gifted her with a smile. "We know."

"Is everybody in on it but me?" Standing in spite of orders to the contrary, Keira gathered the blanket around her and started off across the parking lot. Her feet were still numb and painful beneath the booties the EMTs had given her, as was most of her body, but that didn't matter. She was on a mission. All she cared about was getting back to Nick.

She found him easily by locating the cluster of men surrounding the chief and pushing her way in until she was standing directly in front of her former partner and staring him in the face.

"My turn," she announced with conviction.

Instead of arguing, Aiden opened the rear door of the nearest patrol car and gestured. "If you want to talk, do it where it's warmer. We'll wait right here in case you need us."

Nobody had to invite Keira twice. She slid inside, blanket and all.

Nick followed. "Are you all right?"

She wanted to throw herself into his arms and beg for a thousand kisses. In place of doing that, she convinced herself to answer, "I'm fine. How about you?"

"Hardly a scratch. They tell me Carlton died instantly." His voice wavered. "That could have been you."

"But it wasn't."

"No. I…"

"You did all you could to end a hostage situation, Nick. It's not your fault someone died. That's up to God."

"I like to think so in this case at least. There are times when things like that seem so unfair."

"I know. I felt that way when my mother died. I suppose if we could see into the future, we'd argue with the Lord all the time."

"I suppose so."

His ensuing silence was hard to tolerate, especially since the future was exactly what Keira wanted to discuss. Finally, she tried to draw him out with a softly spoken, "I suppose I have every right to be furious, but I forgive you, Nick."

"For what?"

She had to smile. "Your choice. We could start with your IA assignment and go on from there."

"It's a long list."

"I know. That's okay. I know you had a job to do."

When he reached for her hand, she let him hold it. The warmth of his touch traveled all the way to her heart.

"This is probably a bad time to tell you that I love you," he said.

"The worst." In contradiction to her declaration she was beginning to grin.

"Then I suppose kissing you is out, too."

The fondness in his gaze would have been enough to melt away the last of her anger if she hadn't already put it aside. "Oh, I don't know. You did save my life."

"No, Keira," he whispered, caressing her cheek and leaning closer. "You saved mine. In more ways than I can ever count."

"Then I guess I do deserve a kiss, huh?"

"You certainly do."

Nick's lips claimed hers, gently at first, then with deepening ardor.

Just before she closed her eyes, she saw an intensity in his gaze that rivaled the way he had looked at her when they'd pulled her up from her death grip and she'd crawled into his arms.

Leaning away ever-so-slightly, she pressed her palm to his chest. "I forgot something."

"What?"

There was so much apprehension in his tone, in his expression, she quickly put his mind at ease. "I forgot to tell you that I love you, too."

"Are you sure? We haven't known each other very long."

"No, and I suppose you have all kinds of deep, dark secrets still to tell, but I'll take my chances and stick around to hear them all."

"I'll see that your father gets my real personnel file ASAP."

Cuddling closer, Keira laid her cheek on Nick's chest and listened to the rapid beating of his heart. "I don't need to see any files. I always knew you had to be one of the good guys."

"I am, you know. Even if some of the men in Boston do refer to IA as the Rat Squad."

"That is so wrong. If I were you, I wouldn't want to go back to work there for anything."

Raising her face to look into his eyes, she knew the moment he realized what she was suggesting.

"Your father would never hire me. Not after what's happened."

"Maybe. Maybe not." She giggled. "Why don't you shut up and kiss me again before Dad decides we've *talked* enough and breaks us up?"

That made Nick laugh. "Honey, if a homicidal maniac couldn't break us up, I doubt anybody can."

Satisfied, Keira reached up, slipped her fingers into the short hair at the nape of his neck, pulled him closer and kissed him until she wondered if she was going to swoon for the second time in her life.

EPILOGUE

Dressed in his Fitzgerald Bay Police Department uniform and seated at the desk he still shared with Keira, Nick slapped a sheet of paper onto an existing stack. "There. That's the last form. We're done with Anthony Carlton." He shaped his fingers into a make-believe claw. "Writer's cramp."

She laughed. "From using a keyboard and printer? Sure, Delfino."

"I had to sign them all, didn't I? And speaking of paperwork, are you sure you don't want to read the IA report I submitted?"

"Dad told me the gist of it. You really stuck your neck out when you came to the defense of this department. Thanks."

"I didn't do it because I happen to be in love with you, you know. I really don't think anyone is protecting Charles. I just wish I'd been able to solve the Henry murder and actually *clear* him before my assignment here was complete."

"You mean before the State Police decided you were too biased to be of any more use to them?"

"Yeah. Something like that. I really did think I could continue my undercover work and do a good job somewhere else but my bosses disagreed."

"Their loss is Fitzgerald Bay's gain," Keira told him. "At least Dad didn't hesitate to hire you."

"That shocked me, too, particularly since he knows how you and I feel about each other."

Hesitating, Nick decided this was a good opportunity to tell her about his recent spiritual enlightenment. Even if she laughed, he figured it was high time he stood up for his beliefs.

"Something strange happened to me the night you were kidnapped," Nick said. "I started to believe in God. I mean *really* believe. I even think He answered my prayers when we were at the top of the lighthouse. Does that sound nuts?"

"No," Keira said with tears in her eyes. "It sounds like the answer to my prayers for you."

"Because you didn't like me the way I was?"

She circled the desk and embraced him. "No," she whispered, "because I love you so very, very much."

* * * * *

Dear Reader,

Here we are, once again, in the midst of an ongoing series. This time, my fellow authors and I have brought you to a small coastal town in Massachusetts. The scenery may vary from my usual Arkansas stories but the people aren't really that different at heart. They love each other and many of them love God.

They're also very human, as are we all. Although we may call ourselves Christians, we're nevertheless far from perfect. At least, I know I am. And, by the grace of God, I also know I'm forgiven because I'm His child.

If you aren't sure about your own salvation, just ask in sincere prayer and God will answer.

You can write to me at P.O. Box 13, Glencoe, AR 72539, contact me via my website, www.ValerieHansen.com, or send an email to Val@ValerieHansen.com.

Blessings,

Valerie Hansen

Questions for Discussion

1. In this story, Nick has to actually lie to be honest. Do you understand that concept or does it seem wrong no matter what the extenuating circumstances?

2. When Keira was assigned to be Nick's partner, did you see it as being for her good or not? Might you have thought differently if this was not a romance book?

3. Like many small towns, Fitzgerald Bay has an accepted hierarchy. Does this system seem to help or hinder the official operations? What might work better? Why do you think so?

4. When Olivia Henry was murdered, there was a lot more to the crime than is commonly known. It must have taken tremendous faith and courage for her to leave Ireland and come to a foreign country. Do you think you could ever do something like that? (My own father did!)

5. As Keira starts to have affection for Nick, she doesn't question her feelings even though she hardly knows him. Is that wise? Wouldn't it be smarter for her to keep her distance for a while?

6. It is normally against the rules for relatives to work on the same police department. Can you see why? What problems could have been avoided if Aiden had not hired his sons and daughter?

7. When Keira makes up her mind to become a cop, she faces family opposition. As an obedient daughter, should

she have listened to her father or was she right to follow her heart—and her brothers?

8. Speaking of Keira's brothers, does it seem fair that the family supported them in their careers, yet kept insisting that Keira wasn't suited to the job? That attitude sounds archaic. Is it common these days?

9. Fitzgerald Bay has typical New England charm coupled with bouts of terrible weather. Do you think it would be fun to live in a place like that in spite of the storms? Would the feelings of "home" be worth any sacrifice or not? Why?

10. At the Valentine's party, Nick finally sees Keira dressed up and discovers an attractive woman. She was always pretty. Do you think she was using her uniform to hide behind, like a disguise, to keep herself from romantic entanglements? Or do you think Nick was just dense?

11. With all the modern methods of communication, do you think Fitzgerald Bay is rather backward, or are they simply clinging to a simpler life for the sake of peace and quiet? If there was more open land available so new businesses could be built, would that spoil the whole picture? Why or why not?

12. Nick's job with the Internal Affairs Division makes him unpopular with the officers he busts for crimes. Why aren't others more supportive? Does it make sense that innocent men shun him, too? For what reason?

13. Keira is able to defend herself even when she's freezing and in pain. Have you ever had the kind of experi-

ence where you looked back and wondered how you got through it? Was prayer a help?

14. After Nick makes his report to the State Police and exonerates the Fitzgerald Bay Police Department regarding Charles, is it logical that his former bosses would fire him outright? Might it be smarter for them to simply reassign him? Or is he ruined in regard to that kind of job?

15. When Keira finally hears that Nick has had an epiphany and is learning to trust God, why doesn't she say, "I told you so"? Why would that be unwise? Do you understand her relief and joy? Do you think she needs to do or say anything else at that moment?

INSPIRATIONAL

Wholesome romances that touch the heart and soul.

celebrating
15
YEARS

COMING NEXT MONTH
AVAILABLE MARCH 13, 2012

EYE OF THE STORM
Hannah Alexander

THE DETECTIVE'S SECRET DAUGHTER
Fitzgerald Bay
Rachelle McCalla

BROKEN TRUST
Sharon Dunn

SHADES OF TRUTH
Undercover Cops
Sandra Orchard

REQUEST YOUR FREE BOOKS!

2 FREE RIVETING INSPIRATIONAL NOVELS
PLUS 2 FREE MYSTERY GIFTS

YES! Please send me 2 FREE Love Inspired® Suspense novels and my 2 FREE mystery gifts (gifts are worth about $10). After receiving them, if I don't wish to receive any more books, I can return the shipping statement marked "cancel". If I don't cancel, I will receive 4 brand-new novels every month and be billed just $4.49 per book in the U.S. or $4.99 per book in Canada. That's a saving of at least 22% off the cover price. It's quite a bargain! Shipping and handling is just 50¢ per book in the U.S. and 75¢ per book in Canada.* I understand that accepting the 2 free books and gifts places me under no obligation to buy anything. I can always return a shipment and cancel at any time. Even if I never buy another book, the two free books and gifts are mine to keep forever.

123/323 IDN FEHR

Name	(PLEASE PRINT)	
Address		Apt. #
City	State/Prov.	Zip/Postal Code

Signature (if under 18, a parent or guardian must sign)

Mail to the **Reader Service:**
IN U.S.A.: P.O. Box 1867, Buffalo, NY 14240-1867
IN CANADA: P.O. Box 609, Fort Erie, Ontario L2A 5X3

Not valid for current subscribers to Love Inspired Suspense books.

**Are you a subscriber to Love Inspired Suspense
and want to receive the larger-print edition?
Call 1-800-873-8635 or visit www.ReaderService.com.**

* Terms and prices subject to change without notice. Prices do not include applicable taxes. Sales tax applicable in N.Y. Canadian residents will be charged applicable taxes. Offer not valid in Quebec. This offer is limited to one order per household. All orders subject to credit approval. Credit or debit balances in a customer's account(s) may be offset by any other outstanding balance owed by or to the customer. Please allow 4 to 6 weeks for delivery. Offer available while quantities last.

Your Privacy—The Reader Service is committed to protecting your privacy. Our Privacy Policy is available online at www.ReaderService.com or upon request from the Reader Service.

We make a portion of our mailing list available to reputable third parties that offer products we believe may interest you. If you prefer that we not exchange your name with third parties, or if you wish to clarify or modify your communication preferences, please visit us at www.ReaderService.com/consumerschoice or write to us at Reader Service Preference Service, P.O. Box 9062, Buffalo, NY 14269. Include your complete name and address.

LISUS11B

Victoria Evans has come back to Fitzgerald Bay after ten years, and she's got a secret that will affect one of the Fitzgerald brothers greatly.
Read on for a sneak preview of
THE DETECTIVE'S SECRET DAUGHTER
by Rachelle McCalla, the next exciting book in the
FITZGERALD BAY *series.*

A police cruiser tore up Main Street in Fitzgerald Bay, lights flashing.

Victoria Evans glanced back over her shoulder from the doorway of the Hennessy Law office. Who was in trouble now? She half expected the patrol car to stop in front of the police station, but it skidded to a halt on the other side of the street, and a uniformed officer leaped out, running toward the Sugar Plum Inn and Café.

"My shop!" Victoria turned to face Cooper Hennessy, handing off the frosted cookies she'd walked up the street to deliver. "Paige is in there."

Immediately afraid for her nine-year-old daughter's safety, Victoria leaped from the stoop and sprinted down the street, reaching her front door just as the police officer, who'd darted around the side of the building, circled back to the front.

Victoria reached for the door handle the same instant he did. Gloved fingers brushed her hands. She looked up past the broad shoulders to close-cropped brown hair. The handsome face turned toward her with eyes as blue as the Massachusetts sky. She knew those eyes too well.

"You can't go in there," the officer warned.

Her heart plummeted to her stomach. "But my daughter—"

"She's okay. She called 9-1-1. I don't want you contaminating the crime scene." He turned away and rushed inside.

Tumultuous emotions broke like waves inside her heart. She'd already had a crime scene at the Sugar Plum Inn and Café a few weeks before—an ugly break-in that had caused expensive damages.

What now? Was Paige really okay? Victoria had no family left besides Paige. She had to force herself to follow the officer's instructions not to go inside.

It didn't help who the officer was.

Owen Fitzgerald.

Of all the officers on the Fitzgerald Bay Police Department, why did Owen have to come? She couldn't have him finding out that he had a daughter this way.

Can Victoria and Owen move beyond the past to build a future, or will she become the next target of the killer that is stalking Fitzgerald Bay?

Read THE DETECTIVE'S SECRET DAUGHTER
by Rachelle McCalla to find out.

SHLISEXP0312